D0864673

# LEGACY

*Book 2*
## THE CHRONICLES OF THE NUBIAN UNDERWORLD

Dear Reader:

Shakir Rashaan continues his erotically charged journey in *Legacy*. The true practitioner of the BDSM culture in Atlanta's Fetish community exposes the lifestyle of the Nubian Underworld through his characters.

Ramesses, his wife, Neferterri, and their submissives continue the ride by stepping up the pace in this follow-up to *The Awakening*. After inheriting the "Palace" from his mentor, Amenhotep, Ramesses names it NEBU and puts a plan into action to expand the tradition with compounds in other states. Readers witness from a collaring ceremony of a submissive to the highlights of a phone sex line. They experience the relationships of dominants and submissives, and their world of both pleasure and pain. It's a breathtaking trip to the "dark side" that is unforgettable and full of surprises.

Be sure to check out Shakir's next title in the series, *Tempest*, in which he expects to turn it up yet another notch.

As always, thanks for supporting myself and the Strebor Books family. We strive to bring you the most cutting-edge, out-of-the-box material on the market. You can find me on Facebook @AuthorZane or you can email me at zane@eroticanoir.com.

Blessings,

*Zane*

Publisher
Strebor Books
www.simonandschuster.com

ALSO BY SHAKIR RASHAAN
*The Awakening*

# ZANE PRESENTS

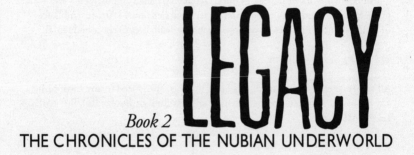

# LEGACY

*Book 2*
## THE CHRONICLES OF THE NUBIAN UNDERWORLD

A NOVEL

# SHAKIR RASHAAN

STREBOR BOOKS

NEW YORK  LONDON  TORONTO  SYDNEY

Strebor Books
P.O. Box 6505
Largo, MD 20792
http://www.streborbooks.com

ISBN 978-1-59309-546-8
ISBN 978-1-4767-4879-5 (ebook)
LCCN 2014931189

First Strebor Books trade paperback edition June 2014

Cover design: www.mariondesigns.com
Cover photograph: © Keith Saunders Photos

10 9 8 7 6 5 4 3 2 1

Manufactured in the United States of America

For information regarding special discounts for bulk purchases, please contact Simon & Schuster Special Sales at 1-866-506-1949 or business@simonandschuster.com

The Simon & Schuster Speakers Bureau can bring authors to your live event. For more information or to book an event, contact the Simon & Schuster Speakers Bureau at 1-866-248-3049 or visit our website at www.simonspeakers.com.

*To My Beloved,*
*United in battle, until death do we part...*
*Most men prefer a Queen, but I'm not most men, I prefer an Empress.*
*I love you.*

# ACKNOWLEDGMENTS

Man, I don't know if you're ready for what's coming!

Well, on second thought, I think I have an idea with some of my readers and supporters, LOL!

Okay, let me get this part out of the way first. I got some things to say once I'm done.

This is (somewhat) a work of fiction. That means that some of this stuff was made up, and some of it includes players whose names have been changed to protect the (not so) innocent. (But you already knew that, remember THE AWAKENING?)

Trust me when I say that the next installment, TEMPEST, is already being polished up for its debut in December. I gotta keep it hotter with every page I write!

I'm starting to get a little deeper, bit by bit, piece by piece, into the Underworld of WIITWD, and I've tried to inspire new things as opposed to just kicking in the same old stuff. Now, for the mainstream "vanilla" folks, this second book might be more than what you can stand, but I promise you it will keep you enthralled and hot! For those that are in the know, you know that I've only scratched the surface, and as the layers are peeled away, you'll love where I'm going with this series.

I used the last book to thank all the folks who really have been in my corner, my family, my friends in and out of the BDSM lifestyle, so I'm taking this opportunity to thank a whole gang of folks who I couldn't get to the last time around, m'kay?

To my literary "wife," N'Tyse, thank you for being my guide in this literary journey, and helping me make the right moves in this industry. Love you, baby!!!

To Zane and Charmaine, the success that I have been able to garner would not have been possible had you not given the thumbs-up and said that this series had potential to do big things. I hope to continue to give you quality projects in a way that only I can bring!

To the reviewers who gave my books a chance: Orsayor Simmons and Book Referees, Johnathan Royal and Books, Beauty and Stuff, Tiffany Tyler and Tiffany Talks Books, OOSA Online Book Club, Michelle Monkou and *USA Today*'s Happy Ever After, and a host of others through the years that read the book and saw the potential and the quality and gave unbiased reviews, thank you so much for helping me grow as a writer and building a relationship with you. I hope to continue giving you books you can brag about to your readers.

To my die-hard readers and supporters, I know there's a LOT more of you with the success of *The Awakening*, but a special thanks goes out to Nikki Cohen, Alexandrea Ward, Joanne Holah, Sophie Sealy, Antoinette Lakey, Areya Branxton-Chase and Latoya Sanlin, the ladies who have been helping me and my Beloved run the Temples of NEBU Facebook group. Thank you for helping me build my brand while I continue to enhance the "Shakir Experience" and expand the "NEBU Universe" for readers and supporters, new and old alike. I would be remiss if I didn't say thank you to you all.

As usual, I know I'm missing a whole gang of folks, so just do me a favor and insert your name in this next statement:

I'd like to thank _____ for the support and love. I hope to continue to put books out that you will want to tell your friends and family about.

Thank you again, and enjoy *Legacy*.

The best legacy I can leave my children is free speech, and the example of using it.

—*Sir Phillip Sidney*

# INTRODUCTION

Welcome back, folks, I hope you enjoyed the initial exploration into the Nubian Underworld. I had good time showing you how things can go, good and bad, while educating and titillating. It's what I do!

If you thought *The Awakening* was a fun ride, wait until you see what I have in store for you with *Legacy*.

When I last left you at the end of *The Awakening*, there was an inner circle present in Dubai to witness the union of my Mentor Amenhotep and His slave paka as husband and wife. You also witnessed some relationships solidify, while others have been regretfully and painfully broken.

Side note: if you're getting ready to read *Legacy* right now and you haven't read *The Awakening* yet, you might wanna put *Legacy* down and read *The Awakening* first, or you won't know what the hell I'm talking about.

So, now that we're all back in the States, I guess we've all tried to get back to some semblance of normalcy. Our newest submissive's name has changed, having gone through the consideration period with Neferterri and me. Kitana is now sajira. Her husband, Ice, is still going through the process with his Domina, Mistress Sinsual. My home boy, Jay, has gotten together with my now former "concubine," Candy, which I can't be too mad about. Besides,

Candy will always be "Daddy's girl," of course. There are some other additions on the horizon as well, but you'll have to read on to find out what may come up.

Neferterri is also breaking in a new male submissive as well, Damian. It has been a very interesting six months indeed.

Neferterri and I have inherited the Palace and what would amount to a small fortune from Amenhotep to take care of the live-in slaves and upkeep of the estate. It has given us the ability to take care of some family matters with the kids and some business ventures as well, including Liquid Paradise. Life is good, definitely, and it has my Beloved and I looking to do some really big things coming into the New Year. When you have millions of dollars to invest and make work for you, the sky is the limit. I'm wondering if my Mentor will like the new additions to the estate and the grounds.

I thought I would allow our little one her own voice, as part of her personal growth with us. Throughout this particular series, starting with Legacy and perhaps beyond, she'll be able to tell her story, if she's a good girl.

Now, to give you a premise for the book you're about to read now, *Legacy*.

With Amenhotep gone from the local POC scene, a transition begins, and everyone in the community is trying to get used to the idea of the power shift within the Atlanta BDSM POC community. Some were okay with it, others obviously not, but that's how the scene goes sometimes. I made sure to stay aware of whatever might arise and that no one tried to slip in and try to throw a monkey wrench in the plans I had. What plans might those be? Well, I guess you'll have to find out, won't you?

In the meantime, I need to leave you now. I have a few business ventures I need to check on and a collaring ceremony to prepare for.

Oh, I'm betting you're wondering about the phone call I got in Dubai. Well, you'll have to read on to find out what that was all about.

Enjoy the ride. I know I will.

# SPECIAL NOTE TO READERS

*The grammatical errors that you might see in dialogue are not over-sights, as it is the popular text and reverence used in some facets of the BDSM world.*

# PROLOGUE ⚵ RAMESSES

"So, how did You enjoy Your time in Dubai, youngster?"

Under normal circumstances, a phone call at 7:00 a.m. wouldn't have bothered me, but coming home and suffering serious jet lag from the near fifteen-hour flight made this phone call something of a cruel joke Amenhotep was playing on me.

With the way I felt, I was in desperate need of a vacation from our vacation. We'd spent nearly a week in paradise, one of the most unique and luxurious locales on the planet while celebrating His and paka's nuptials, and here He was sounding bright-eyed and bushy-tailed like the flight time never had one ounce of an effect on Him.

I looked at the phone, trying my best to match His energy, realizing quickly that I wouldn't come close to meeting Him halfway. "Dubai was wonderful, and that's putting it mildly, Sir." I did my best to clear up the grogginess in my voice before I spoke again. My voice sounded like I'd gargled with broken glass. "I feel so drained right now. If I were working for someone else, I would be calling in sick. Why are You calling so early in the morning anyway, Sir? Is something wrong?"

"Well, to answer Your question, we have business to take care of, kid." He sounded as serious as a heart attack as His voice carried through the air waves and into my ears. "Oh, and You are working for someone else…You're working for Me, now."

His trademark chuckle made me want to vomit. He couldn't be serious about trying to get back to business now, could He?

"Come on, Sir? Give Me twenty-four hours to recover, veg out on the couch and enjoy the children, anything other than working the next morning after we'd gotten off the plane?" I hated sounding like a freaking teenager trying to beg his father for more time to be lazy, but I really needed some time to be lazy. Neferterri was soundly sleeping next to me, completely oblivious to the conversation I was having with Him.

Why in the hell did I have to be a light sleeper?

The laughter over the phone after I made my plea gave me the distinct impression that my request would not be honored. "See, that's the problem with you young folks. By now, I would have taken care of the things that we need to take care of before lunch. Are You getting soft on Me already, youngster?"

I sat up after hearing that question. "Not by a long shot, old man, but I have to wonder how in the world You're able to be so fucking hyper when You took the same flight we took to get back home?"

"Clean living, You should try it sometime." His voice never lost its energy. Slowly and surely, it began to breathe life into me, providing the necessary adrenaline rush to lift from the bed and shuffle into the bathroom to begin freshening up. "In order to be great, You have to leave Your mark. Are You ready to leave Your mark, Ramesses?"

He appealed to my ego with that question. He knew full well I was ready to leave my mark, and I was ready to do it in a *big* way. I had been plotting and planning ever since the conversation we had in Dubai one night, when everything was set in motion:

*"I'm ready to do this, Sir. The shock has worn off. It's My time, now."*

*"Is that right, Ramesses? Do You think You're ready to take things to the next level?"*

"I wouldn't be here talking with You if I wasn't ready to take things to the next level. The question is, are You ready for what the next level is?"

"Youngster, I've been waiting for You for the past few years to figure out when You were ready. I have the means for You to do what needs to be done, and You have the energy and drive

to make it all happen. The way I see it, it's a win-win proposition for everyone involved."

"So, why are we here talking when we can be laying the groundwork so I can hit the ground running when we get back? You know the expansion plans I've wanted to execute for some time now."

"The answer to Your question comes with its own question, Ramesses. The plans for the Palace are only the tip of the iceberg. There's something else I need You to do for Me. This is big, probably bigger than any plans You might have for the Palace."

"I haven't refused You before, what makes You think I'm backing down from this request?"

"The request I am making of You, Sir, will require You to do something that I don't know if You're going to be willing to do."

"Stop speaking in riddles and get to the point, Sir. You know I don't do the cloak-and-dagger nonsense. Spit it out."

"In order for You to accomplish the expansion plans that You have in mind, You're going to have to have two individuals to help with those plans. They haven't spoken to each other in nearly a decade, and despite My efforts, they have yet to reach an accord. Where I have failed, perhaps You might succeed. It's the only way Your ultimate plans will come to fruition."

"If it's the two people that I think You're talking about, Sir, I might as well scrap the plans now."

"Don't be so quick to scrap what has been laid out for You, Ramesses. You and I both know things happen for a reason."

"I'm dying to know what the reason is for this one."

"*Only time will tell, My old friend…only time will tell.*"

"You haven't answered My question, kid," Amenhotep's voice sliced through my thoughts. "Are You ready to leave Your mark?"

What He asked for was the impossible. A decade of noncommunication and animosity, and I was supposed to diffuse that in the course of months? If He couldn't do it, what made Him think I would be able to do it?

Yes, I have an ego bigger than the great state of Texas, but even I have my limitations. On the one hand, what He was asking for was next to impossible, but on the other hand, if I had the right leverage, I might have the ability to do something my Mentor wasn't able to do. The end game was too seductive to resist.

"I'm ready, Sir," I answered. "And I already have a plan in mind."

# ONE ⚭ SAJIRA

The headset I wore felt like it had become a chain, weighing me down against my will. Thanks to my Daddy, I hadn't minded chains much anymore. What had begun as fun, sitting on the phone at home and talking dirty to anonymous men, knowing I was getting them off with a slutty voice and filthy language, had fallen into a mundane pattern.

The monotony started when I started spending most of my time screaming, *"Oh yeah, baby, fuck me in my ass"* to men whose wives or girlfriends refused to satisfy their fantasy of anal sex, and quite frankly, I didn't get it. I absolutely enjoyed it, especially with my Daddy. Damn, I got chills thinking about it.

Oh, and let's not forget the "hetero-flexible" men, either. All they ever wanted to talk about was fucking guys who looked like girls, so, on those calls, I pitched my voice deep and pretended to be a horny transvestite, and even with this variation, I still spent most of the time screaming, *"Oh yeah, your cock is so big up my ass, baby."*

Yeah, right. At least I could take pride in the fact that I could manipulate my voice to be whatever they needed me to be. While it was a lot of fun doing that, it became its own problem to maintain the motivation.

Okay, before you go there and tell them I've been a bad girl, my

Daddy and my Goddess know about the side gig. In fact, they encouraged it as part of my slut training. In their minds, it was a welcome contrast in style to my accounting career during the day. So, before you think about going to tell on me, I figured I needed to drop that bit of information on you. Besides, they'll only look at you like you're nuts for telling them what they already know.

Believe me, they…know…*everything*.

Anyway, there's one caller, we'll call him "George." His calls were probably the only calls I actually dreaded, and he called at least once a night, sometimes it would be six or seven times a night, and it was sick and repetitive what he wanted to talk about. The funny thing was he always wanted to try and dominate me, be his little bitch.

Only one man had that power over me, and it's not my husband.

It was easy to get him riled up whenever he tried that mess with me. Neferterri always told me guys like that usually had no power in their own lives, so they used a chat line or phone sex line to regain some sort of balance. It was pathetic, in my opinion, but sometimes you had to do what you had to do to get by. I was glad I didn't have to do it.

I was daydreaming about Neferterri when the beep came over my line again. It was so vivid, I had trouble getting into character. "This is Tina, your sex goddess. Can I verify that you are over eighteen, please, before we continue this phone call?"

"Don't worry, Tina," the caller said. "I think I more than qualify."

The caller had a deep voice, but it was soft also, possessing a hint of ruffneck around the edges. It seemed to travel over the phone line and almost invaded every one of my senses, like he was in the room with me. I didn't pay it much attention, though. All I worried about was finishing this call as soon as possible, so I could get some rest before my husband came home from work.

"Hello, caller, may I have your name, please?" I asked.

"No, Tina, you may not." The silky-smooth, masculine voice was so sexy it always had me wondering if there was a body to match every time he called. His answer still perturbed me, nearly pissing me off because he wouldn't participate in the burgeoning fantasy playing out in my mind. I wanted to give him his money's worth, but he was fucking up a wet dream in the making.

"So, what shall I call you, sir?" I asked again, sticking to the script when dealing with assholes that wanted to play a role. God, all he had to do was play along and we could both get off.

"I think you have figured it out," he answered. The enigmatic tone in his voice intrigued me and repulsed me at the same time.

"You want me to call you 'sir'?" I questioned. I tried to keep my wits about me, but this guy was turning me off by the second. I was going to have to pull an Academy Award-winning performance with this one.

"That's right, Tina, I want you to call me 'sir.' How old are you, Tina, and tell me the truth; I will know if you don't." He was insistent, almost controlling, as he inquired.

In truth, I couldn't call him a mystery, or even a stranger, for that matter. He had been calling for about the past month or so, and he always called me on the same days, but not often enough to where I could figure out when he was calling so that I could be prepared for his call. Sometimes the calls would be hot as hell, to the point to where I needed to masturbate again between calls. Other times, it would be a test of my patience before he finally got off. But it seemed as if he was doing enough to keep me interested and repulsed at the same time.

But, whatever, it's not like this dude had a polygraph over the phone or something. "I'm nine..."

"The truth, Tina, you are never supposed to tell me anything but the truth," he demanded. "I can hear the maturity in your voice; you're older than nineteen."

"I'm twenty-three, sir." I lied anyway, this time a little more demurely to keep up the façade of my "submission" to him. I didn't care who the person was, the one thing I never do, and what the company that I work for requires, is to give my real name, age, or location.

"And what is your real name, Tina?" he asked. I noticed more aggression in his voice this time. I swear this guy wouldn't quit. I didn't care how turned on I was with him in the past, I was two seconds shy of disconnecting the line, but not before I milked him for what he was worth.

"I'm sorry, sir?"

"Your real name, bitch...*now!*"

"It's Melissa, sir," I snapped as the fake name rolled off my tongue like it was my real name. Yeah, I was really going to tell him my real name; who the hell was he kidding? He had me mixed up with another clueless bitch or something. He wouldn't know if I was lying or telling the truth anyway; I was on a secured line. Daddy made sure of it before I started working.

"Melissa, I understand, not exactly a sexy name. I'll call you Calypso instead. Will you be my Calypso?" His voice deepened.

At last, I was relieved, some type fantasy, someone I could "be" for this jackass. "Certainly, sir, I'll be your Calypso."

"Do you live alone, Calypso? Remember, tell the truth."

"No sir, I don't." I blew out air in frustration, muting my headset to keep him from hearing it. This dude was getting too personal. I should have hung up the phone then, but this was more of a power play now, and he was not about to get the best of me.

"Who do you live with, Calypso?"

"I live with my boyfriend, sir."

"And is he good to you; does he take good care of you? Does he turn you on?"

"Sir?" I asked. I didn't want to engage in unnecessary drivel, but I was gonna get my money out of him. Thank goodness it was almost time for me to get off work anyway, otherwise, I would have cut his ass a long time ago.

"This is *my* time, Calypso. Never give me anything but your full attention during *my* time." The tone in his voice tried to give me the idea he wanted to get rough with me.

"Yes sir." I couldn't argue with him, nor did I want to. He was right after all, it was his time…and his dime. "I'm yours for as long as you like."

"Calypso, does your boyfriend take care of you?"

"No sir, he…well, he can barely hold down a job."

"And does he turn you on?"

"No sir, mostly he bores me." I knew full well I was getting satisfied on a lot of levels, but he didn't need to know all of that information. All I needed was another ten minutes with him and I would have gotten my c-note out of him for the night.

"What turns you on, Calypso?"

"Ummm…" The "shy girl" persona kicked in now; my eyes watching the clock the entire time.

"Does this job do it for you?" he asked with contempt.

"No sir, nothing really does anymore." I was mentally done with him, now. My body didn't even want to respond to anything he said. I wanted to say, "You don't do it for me," but I knew that wouldn't help matters for getting the money out of him I wanted.

"Mmmmmm, I'm sure we can find something, Calypso." I imagined the smirk on his face as he mumbled those words.

"Yes sir, I'm sure." I was ad-libbing now, preparing to launch into my "fuck me up the ass" persona because this guy was boring me to tears.

"Don't patronize me, Calypso. I want you, but I want you willing, and I want you mine, completely mine. I'm not interested in your professional self, your phone self. I want *you*, Calypso; do you understand that?"

"Yes sir." I was surprised at my response. It felt almost like enthusiasm for a moment. I heard him getting excited, which meant I could milk him some more. That got me wet, releasing my inner slut.

"That's better, pet. Now tell me what you look like for real. I want you to stand in front of a mirror and tell me what you see."

I knew from his tone he was serious, but I was snug in my bed and horny. There wasn't a force on earth that could get me out of bed...well, that's not entirely accurate.

"Well, I'm about five feet seven inches, reddish-brown hair, light-green eyes..."

"What is your body like, my dear?"

"Well, it's not perfect; I could lose about fifteen pounds, but it is not bad, either. I have forty-four-inch hips, a thirty-two-inch waist, and I measure 38C at the bust."

It's amazing what you could come up with when money was a motivating factor. I actually got wetter by the minute, feeding into the role play as the time ticked away. My body looked nothing like the way I described, but I went with what the customer might like, and it's what seemed to work for him.

"Do you understand you are mine?"

Oh yeah, I understood. I was "his," even if this was the one time I would speak to him tonight because he would never get a whiff of me...I was "his."

Until he began having conversations with the dial tone after I hung up.

"Yes sir, I understand. I am yours."

"Then put your hand down your pants and play with your pussy."

I hesitated a moment and considered my options. By then, thoughts of Ramesses invaded my mind, and I heard his voice in my head, replacing the one in my ear. My legs slowly parted, and at my Daddy's commands in my ear, I started playing with my clit. I got quiet for a minute, almost forgetting I was on the line with my wannabe domi-*not*.

"Calypso," he growled softly. "you are *mine*, period. Now put your hands down your pants and play with your pretty pussy."

I don't think he understood what was going on, and I didn't care. The only voice in my head was Daddy's and my fingers worked their magic like they had other forces controlling them. My fingers felt the slick wetness as I slowly slipped into my own private mind fuck.

"I want you to rub it very slowly in a circular motion," he told me. I still ignored him, giving out some moans for his benefit, but playing the tune only my Goddess could understand. I felt the softness of my Goddess' hand caressing my skin. He could have called me everything but a child of God and I would have cared less.

I followed his "directions," feeling the satin wetness of my now dripping lips. I let out a soft sigh. *God*, it felt so damn good.

"Calypso, does it feel good?"

"*Mmmm-hmmm…*"

"You will address me as *SIR* and speak with words and not sounds, Calypso. Does it feel good?"

"Yes sir, it feels incredible, sir." I rushed through the response. It didn't matter what he said to me anymore; he was a pending footnote in the story of my growing orgasm. I was on automatic, taking out a dildo to feel something inside me to get me over the edge. I needed my husband to come home at that exact moment, so I could fuck his brains out.

"That's better, my dear. Do you think you can come for me, Calypso?"

"Yes sir, I think I can come for you."

"Don't, baby, enjoy it. Keep it on the edge."

"But sir…I want to come so badly."

"Calypso, we agreed you are mine, *and as such ,you will not come!!!!!!*"

"Yes sir," I told him over the phone, but I hovered over my clit, enjoying the sensations, the energy that pulsated from it.

"Calypso, what is your phone number?"

"757-215-7731, sir." I may have been in orgasmic bliss, but I was not stupid. My Goddess taught me well.

"What city do you live in, Calypso?"

"Norfolk, sir, I live in Norfolk, Virginia."

"Very good, now, stop."

Hell no, I wasn't going to stop. My hands were working at a feverish pace by then, and I was just about to come when…

"Calypso…"

"Sir?"

"I'll be coming for you soon." His tone chilled me. It wasn't the "oh baby, I'm about to come" type of phrase, but something that stopped me in mid-stroke.

Before I could respond, the line went dead.

# TWO ⊗ NEFERTERRI

"So, let Me get this straight, so I don't have this mixed up. We're going public with the Palace?"

I looked into my husband's eyes as we walked into the currently constructed home soon to replace the house we were in the process of renting out to family members.

"No, babe, we're not exactly going public; it's more like, semi-public," Ramesses answered, taking in the larger space we would soon be moving into. "There are some rules to this new idea I have. In fact, if it works, we may very well be duplicating this idea in different parts of the country."

I hated when he pulled the secrecy nonsense with me. Ever since Amenhotep left, my husband had been more engaged into the comings and goings within the Atlanta BDSM community, and that's saying a lot, considering we were already "plugged in" to begin with. But then again, considering that we're both entrepreneurs now, instead of working in Corporate America full time, some priorities could be readjusted and balances could be struck. During the day, since the kids were in school, it's easy to get some marketing and other business conducted. I managed to talk both my mother and my mother-in-law into retiring from their jobs and share the responsibility of taking the kids to their respective extracurricular activities, for operating expenses and "mad money," so to speak. They were more than happy to take retirement and use the money we were giving them to do with what they wanted.

I got used to the idea of having a lot of businesses to handle. We had begun the process of opening a daycare center, a mail center, and we expanded my husband's photography studio to include not only commercial work for his former apprentice, but to open the possibilities for doing fetish work also. Combine that with Liquid Paradise, and now the idea of turning the Palace into a "bondage ranch" type of compound started to get my juices flowing.

There would definitely not be a dull moment, that's for sure, and all of it had been bankrolled, thanks to Amenhotep wanting to make sure that His extended family was taken care of. Not to mention, making more money for Him. After all, He was a businessman above all else.

The other idea I had to get used to was enjoying our submissives, without the time constraints that working a normal nine-to-five demanded. I mean, don't get me wrong, I enjoyed both our girls when they were in our care and charge. But there was something different about the interaction that sajira and I had. It felt deeper somehow, like we'd done this dance before some time ago, and I don't mean a few years, either. All I knew was it was going to be an interesting ride, to say the least.

Damian, on the other hand, was a little easier to figure out. With him, everything seemed to ebb and flow so smoothly between us, and he was definitely picking up on my patterns and tastes quite nicely, indeed.

Despite all of the positive things that were happening, I really missed my shamise. She would really flourish in this new atmosphere.

But for now, I needed a few answers from my husband regarding the plans for the *Palace* since that was the one business that I had the least amount of "hands on" direct contact with, just as he allowed me to run Liquid the way I saw fit while choosing to remain a silent partner. I trusted the decisions and vision, but I was a nosey bitch, so sue me.

"So what are these new rules You had in mind?" I tried to refocus a little bit before my mind wandered to places I didn't need to be at that exact moment.

"Cell phones will be checked at the gate, and no cameras, for starters," Ramesses stated, and I saw the gears turning in his mind, as if he were doing the usual mental checklist. "The security detail will tell the concierges of any messages that are left on the cell phones, and they will then pass the message to the member. Cell phones will be tagged with the member's name, or pseudonym. Dom will head up the detail, as well as the security firm that I'm creating."

Did he say security firm? That detail wasn't lost on me, but I didn't expect him to head into that direction. "Wait a minute; what's this talk about a security firm?"

Ramesses smiled. "I'm planning on talking Dom into retirement."

"I'd love to be a fly on the wall of that conversation." I tried to stifle a giggle, forcing myself to stay involved with the conversation instead, resisting the urge to make comedic remarks. "I thought he was all in with the force? Isn't he a detective now?"

Ramesses smirked before puffing out his cheeks, trying to resemble Marlon Brando in *The Godfather*. "I'm going to make him an offer he can't refuse," he stated as he mimicked the fictional Don Corleone. "But You shouldn't worry about such things, Beloved. Before it's over, I'll have what I want."

I couldn't stop laughing at his attempt to be theatrical as I started making my own to-do list in my head in case he missed anything. "What else?"

"Rather than do any real advertising online or going through publications, we're going to go back to word-of-mouth building of clientele. We can't let it get too far out of hand, or we'll end up with a faction we don't want, and they'll screw it up for the rest of us," he continued. "I'm also thinking of setting up charter members and a council to handle legal issues and rules violations, etcetera. Of course, it would consist of a few of the regular members in its charter stage, and after the first year, elected council members will serve on the council. I was thinking of Mistress Sinsual, Mistress Blaze, Master Altar, and You and I, and one of the more trusted submissives to round out the six-member council. Also, having people in charge of the membership dues as well as executing penalties for violating nondisclosure agreements. If You name it, we need to have it executed. I want to make sure we have the bases covered so we don't get burned."

"Okay, I'm with You so far, baby." I continued scribbling away in shorthand, making other mental notes, thinking of the other things we need to do to duplicate a lot of the safeguards we had in place at Liquid. "Is there anything else? Are we keeping the operating hours for the weekend?"

"Yes, and I want to hire kink-friendly people to work the weekends, at a worthwhile rate, of course. I was also thinking we could get with the bondage manufacturers to send reps in to sell their products, do product demos, with those members willing to do the demos in exchange for a discounted rate on their membership dues for the month." He kept rattling the information off at a steady pace. I looked on as he continued assessing the details in his photographic memory. "The dues, I want to keep at a moderate rate, at least for now, because we don't want to alienate anyone who might want to enjoy the Palace. But if membership starts to rise a bit, we'll have to make a decision on crowd control. We don't want this thing to get too big, to where we draw too much attention."

"But if we get too big, then what about extra accommodations at a hotel nearby or something like that? Perhaps we can negotiate a rate or something?" I asked. The way things were at the Palace right now, a small contingent could stay overnight. But what happened if the Palace couldn't hold everyone that wanted to stay?

"Well, Beloved, since we currently have a good three hundred acres to mess around with, I've been a bit busy with an expansion project to get things in motion." Ramesses smirked. "Actually, to be correct, I have a few projects going on simultaneously out there right now. Once we're done making sure this house is squared away, We can go by there so You can see what's going on, if You'd like?"

"Wait a minute; did You say *expansion?*" I asked, raising an eyebrow.

"Yes, darling, expansion." He gave me a look that shut me down. I enjoyed being a Domina, but sometimes, that look kept me balanced, I swear. "I've already sent the plans out to Amenhotep, if You're wondering, babe. I don't do much without Him knowing about it, especially when it comes to His properties."

Actually, that wasn't exactly what was on my mind, but Amenhotep was old school. One of the things about the Palace He liked was the fact that, despite its size, it was still somewhat humble and quaint in His eyes, and He also liked that it didn't draw too much attention to itself, despite its ominous size. I was worried that perhaps the semi-publicity might be a little upsetting to Him.

I decided to wait until we actually got to the Palace before I made any more assumptions. Besides, I might have liked what I saw and taken things to the next level myself.

☥

It was absolutely breathtaking…

Seeing all the construction around the *Palace* was absolutely breathtaking, and yet overwhelming at the same time. I saw several buildings in a bed-and-breakfast-style architecture laid out in a strategic manner.

After touring the finished house, I took inventory of the how the rest of the buildings would be laid out: none of the houses would be more than two floors in height, and lavishly constructed with a common area and five to seven rooms on the ground floor, and ten more rooms on the second floor per building.

In all, Ramesses had gotten permits for thirteen houses, about 200-plus rooms on the grounds in total.

This resembled more and more a compound than an estate, and I wondered if it was what Ramesses had in mind when he began these projects. He said before that he was thinking big, but I had no idea. But, this was his baby, his business venture, and I was content he was moving in the proper direction.

We finally got to the main building, and I was relieved to see that it had remained unscathed. There were no scaffolds around it or anything. I was relieved that Ramesses had no intentions of making any changes. We got out of the car and began to walk around the buildings closest to the main building.

"So, what do You think?" He stood with me in front of the completed housing, gauging my response to his question.

"I'm speechless," I admitted. The grounds were absolutely gorgeous. "Can any of the buildings be seen from the street?"

"No, I made sure they were strategically placed within the landscaping and the woods as well. The only way someone will be able to see anything would be by helicopter." He stroked his beard for a moment, snapping out of it when he realized he had one last thing on his mind. "The only thing the place needs is a new name."

"What name did You have in mind?" I asked him. "I'm assuming it's got a meaning, knowing You."

"NEBU." The name rolled off his tongue, and he had this smirk on his face, anticipating my confusion.

"Where did the name 'NEBU' come from?"

"It represents the Palace of Gold from the ancient Kingdom," he said. "I want to present the new compound in its splendor."

"I like the name, it works for Me. Have You told sajira and Damian about it?" I asked.

"No, not yet, but I think it would be nice for them to see it as well, considering they will be helping with the hosting duties and such. Actually, I want to bring sajira on to the payroll full time, now that I think about it." He grinned at the possibilities ahead. "I know she would love to be able to set her own hours for a change, work with some larger figures and P&L's."

I couldn't get too excited, well, actually I could, but it was more of excitement for sajira than for Damian. sajira was a collared submissive of the House now, so she would be involved in the operations of NEBU. I was happy about that. I wasn't sure if I was ready to bring Damian along, though. He had yet to prove himself to the other members of the House.

"I don't mind sajira seeing this, but Damian's another issue, baby," I told my husband. "He's become more slut than submissive, and he hasn't shown any signs of trying to come out of that phase."

"So, the question I have for You is, what do You want to do with him?" Ramesses asked. "You and I both know he is of no use to Me if he isn't at least a service slave."

I honestly wanted to hold out hope Damian would work out, but every conversation we had as of recent was revolving around his foot fetishes. That was fine for a day or so in the beginning, but ultimately, his purpose was and would always be to please me as I saw fit, and I was no one's Pro Domme.

"I may have to put him to the test, to see if he is truly ready to be a part of this House, baby," I finally stated.

"Good, because I know at least five slaves at NEBU who have been dying for You to acquire them." Ramesses chuckled, seeming to be amused at the whole situation. I wasn't amused by his chiding. I wanted his support in dealing with Damian, the same as I did with our former submissives, jamii and nuru.

Whatever...I have no problems working this out to my benefit. I'd show him he wasn't the only one who could train.

"Changing the subject, I think it's time we give our little one a proper ceremony, don't You think?" Ramesses asked me. "I mean, it's only a matter of completing the circle, such as it is."

He was right, and I was already a step ahead of him this time. "I've already made the arrangements with Altar for two weeks from now. I'm assuming You can have this compound presentable by then, Beloved?"

He flinched for a minute, like he needed to contemplate some figures and dates in his head. I always hated when he did that. I always had to write down dates and details to make sure

I didn't forget, while he simply relied on his photographic memory.

Ramesses stroked his goatee the way he normally did when he had come to a conclusion about something, and then he finally answered, "So shall it be done, Beloved. Do we have the normal guest lists prepared?"

"Yes."

"Then I believe it is time to inform our little one of what she needs to be prepared for then, yes?"

"Oh yes, definitely. I believe she is ready, and it is a wonderful time to do something like this, baby." After all, it was the beginning of the year, and it was time for the local community to take notice of the House of Kemet-Ka once again. Call me arrogant if you want, but even when Amenhotep was there, we still set the standard when it came to stability, especially in the age of "Internet BDSM" and "Velcro collars." The last year might not have proven as such, but a statement must be made again.

We took a final spot check around the grounds before we got back in the truck to head away from NEBU. There was much to plan, phone calls to make, including a special invitation via satellite phone to the Virgin Islands.

"Oh, that reminds Me, I have to fly out in a couple of days," Ramesses said. He anticipated the look on my face, putting his hands up in mock defense. "I have a couple of places I have to go, but I promise I won't be gone longer than about four days."

Here we were with the secrecy and innuendo again. If I didn't know him the way I did, I would have been immediately suspicious of the reason to go on a trip without me. I wanted to ask him a few more questions, but I had a feeling I wouldn't get the answers I wanted to get. At least, I wouldn't get them from him. I knew who I needed to ask, and thankfully, I would be able to pick His brain while asking Him and His newlywed bride to come and see what's going on.

"Okay, Beloved, I'll make sure I call Amenhotep to make sure of a few things." I'd trusted him, even though his "need to know" mantra got on my nerves. But, knowing him, I would find out everything I would need to know when I needed to know it.

Who was I kidding? I didn't have that type of patience.

He raised an eyebrow, recognizing my body language. "Beloved, trust Me on this one. You know I would never keep anything from You without good reason."

In my heart, I trusted what he was saying to me, but it was my mind that needed convincing. The way I saw it, I would have to keep myself busy while he was away, and I had something in mind to accomplish that.

We headed home, with the first thing on my to-do list the moment he took off in the morning being a phone call that might turn into a few revelations, if I had my way…and I *would* have my way.

# THREE ❦ RAMESSES

"That's right. I want to duplicate what I'm planning down in ATL."

I was in Las Vegas chatting with Master Osiris and Lady Hatshepsut, two very longtime friends of Amenhotep and Elders in the Las Vegas BDSM community, laying down the ground work for trying to do a Vegas version of NEBU together out there. They had known Him for the better part of thirty years, since the *Society of Janus* days when they were all in San Francisco together before Amenhotep moved to the East Coast, and the two of them settled into the desert.

"So, what's exactly the plan down in Atlanta, now that Your Mentor has decided to semi-retire?" Osiris asked, stroking his long beard. He had a very unassuming presence, until he stood up. There's something to be said about men who could change the energy flow of a room the moment they stepped into it, and he was one of those men. "I'm hearing the home He left You to renovate to Your style is coming along nicely."

"Yes, Sir, things are going along according to plan. We are obeying the zoning ordinances as we should, and thank goodness the acreage helps with keeping the neighbors out of our hair. I'm also utilizing a KAP lawyer to handle the other sensitive details for membership and the handling of the rules of the ranches," I told him, matching his intense stare as I was taught when I was an apprentice Dominant and I first was introduced to Master Osiris. He was impressed with my usage of a KAP, or kink-aware professional, which the National Coalition of Sexual Freedom established years ago. I had a feeling a non-KAP lawyer wouldn't quite "get" what we were trying to accomplish and might have a few problems… and questions.

Lady Hatshepsut crossed her legs, stroking her pet senmut's head as she waited for us to finish that portion of the conversation. "Where did You plan on placing the Vegas version of NEBU, My dear? For that matter, what did You have in mind for the name of it here?"

I thought about it for a moment, and to be honest, I really didn't expect to get to this point of the conversation. Considering that the Power Exchange was already in the area, I wasn't sure there would be a market for a second major dungeon project. But, it didn't take long for me to come up with the perfect name for the project in Vegas.

"The Temples of Deshret," I responded. I remembered from the ancient Kingdom the name was utilized by the ancient Egyptians to refer to the desert that bordered the country from the west. Deshret means "the Red Land" in Egyptian as well, which also gave me the idea of the color scheme for the project. "That is what I had in mind for the project, m'Lady."

"Brother Amenhotep has taught You well, youngster," Osiris commented. I guess to the Elders I will always be the youngster they helped "raise." I chuckled to myself at that remark, but I was fine with it. In my mind, it was a sign of respect from an Elder to an "offspring." "I wonder how He might react to seeing the renovations to His former home."

I wasn't worried about the renovations. Like I told Neferterri, I sent Him every detail by fax and email through paka, since she was more adept at dealing in the technology age than her husband. Each and every time, the renovations were returned with the customary, "go ahead to get it done."

I wasn't sure if He would be all that pleased with the underground marketing campaign I had planned to wage within the Internet boards and such.

"You shouldn't worry about such things, Master Osiris," I reassured. I took it upon myself to throw the vanity card out there for the two of them to consider. "Besides, I was hoping You would be able to assist Me in the operations here in Vegas with the *Deshret* project? I would want You and m'Lady to, of course. I know Master Amenhotep would trust no one more than the two of You to have the vision to look after one of His business ventures?"

Yeah, I was laying it on thick, but I also knew without the Elders. I'd be better off trying to get the Clarke County Council to approve this project within the Vegas city limits, and I would probably have more success.

"I have already staked out a spot near Mountain Springs, off Route 160," I dropped into business mode with my next statement. "It will be close enough to the airport, and the transportation to and from the compound wouldn't be too much to worry over, especially with the clientele who will be willing to participate in a more discreet location. L.A., San Fran, the folks coming up from Arizona and Central Texas as well. The possibilities would be wonderful to imagine."

That seemed to do the trick, because Lady Hatshepsut spoke up. "We would be delighted to help in this endeavor. You've seemed to have done Your due diligence in getting this project together. What do You need from Us?"

The information flowed out of me with the smoothness of a river. "I know between the two of You, there should be enough people for Me to contact and be willing to put this thing together: legal counsel, security, accounting, the works."

"We're talking high-powered clientele, correct, Ramesses?" Master Osiris asked, no doubt wondering if it would be open to those who had a bit more at stake in the interest of keeping a discretionary profile.

"Affirmative, Sir. Which reminds Me, would You both like to witness Our sajira's collaring ceremony in a couple of weeks? I would imagine You would have a lot of the answers to some lingering questions in Your minds, once You have seen NEBU for Yourselves." I wanted to ensure this wasn't some fly-by-night affair and everything had come to fruition in my home location. There was no point in going out there to pitch the idea if I didn't already have something for them to see.

"That would be wonderful! Is it the one Amenhotep has been raving about, this sajira of Yours?" Lady Hatshepsut asked me.

"Yes, Ma'am, We are quite proud of her indeed."

"We would be delighted. I'll have My boi make the arrangements for our arrival right away."

Just like that, the conversations regarding the birth of The Temples of Deshret began. I wondered if the other leg of my travel itinerary would go this smoothly, especially considering the next person I would have to convince would not be as easy as this had been.

Not only would I have the compound to pitch, but I also would need to broach another subject which could cause the whole plan to fall apart before it all began. Whether it would work out or not was anyone's guess, but nothing beat a try but a failure.

I approached Osiris when we had a chance to speak. "Sir, I might need Your assistance in a matter of the utmost importance."

"Talk to Me, dude, what can I help with?" Osiris asked.

"Well, Sir, it concerns Your brother, Seti." I broached the subject, realizing it needed to be discussed sooner rather than later. "I planned on heading to Virginia in the next couple of days, and I wanted Your counsel on how to deal with Him."

Osiris rubbed the back of his head. I couldn't find a good time to bring up the subject of his brother, but I had to do something, considering I would be on the East Coast in the next forty-eight hours. "I assume there's no one else who could head up this particular project in the area?"

I understood his frustration, but as much as I would have loved to talk to someone else, there was no one else who had the influence and power that Seti had. His circle of friends spanned some of the more well-to-do in the DMV, or the DC/Maryland/Virginia area,

"No, Sir, there's no one else." My options were limited, and I had to make him aware of that fact. As much as I wanted to use someone else, no one had as much influence in the area. "The minute He finds out You're involved in this project, He could pull out completely. I'm sure You know from talking to Amenhotep how important it is not to have that happen."

Osiris clapped his hand on my shoulder, a reassuring smile spread across his face. "Well, youngster, maybe ol' Seti might have softened up a little bit over the past decade. We still talk on occasion, as long as *that* subject doesn't come up. Maybe You might be the one who might be able to work Him over and get Him back within the circle."

Maybe I was, maybe I wasn't…but there was only one way to find out.

# FOUR ⚭ SAJIRA

"What's gotten into you, babe? This isn't the man that I married. What is Sin doing to you?"

I didn't know what to think anymore. Ever since my husband started taking his submission and consideration period with Sinsual more seriously, I'd noticed a change in him, and it wasn't for the better, either.

He wasn't as aggressive in bed as he used to be. I almost had to rape him nowadays. Hell, it's the other part of the reason why I took the part-time phone-sex gig. He'd become meek, almost unsure of himself when he's around any other woman except for his Mistress. I tried to figure out exactly what happened because it had really putting a strain on things.

"Nothing's wrong with me; I've actually never felt more secure with myself." He basked in the afterglow of his orgasmic bliss, giving me a look like he could use a cigarette or two. I wished I could have joined in with him, but he decided the lift off without me. Unfortunately, like the last couple of months since we had gotten back from Dubai, we simply hadn't been in sync sexually.

"So, it's not bothering you that you haven't made me come in a couple of months then, huh?" I retorted. I folded my arms across my naked breasts, glaring at him while he looked at me like I had some nerve even saying something to him. I was wet as hell and ready to fuck my husband again, because he truly still turned me on, but a woman could only take so much.

Ice finally saw the look on my face and realized I was serious, but that didn't change his demeanor. He actually matched my incredulous look with one of his own, like I should have gotten mine while he was getting his.

This shit wasn't cute.

"It never took you this long to come before," he had the nerve to say. "I guess your orgasm control training must be having its effect on you after all."

Low blow, bastard…but that's okay, two can play that game.

"And I see Sin letting you out of your chastity belt to satisfy your wife hasn't worked, either. Maybe I need to have Her put it back on you, since you're not doing anything good with it." Since he wanted to play rough, I had no choice but to hit him where it hurt. With a stone-cold freak like my husband, it meant taking his libido away, which his Domina had seemed to become adept at taking from him, except when he was commanded to fuck her…*well*.

"Now that's fucked up. I worked hard to get that damn thing removed, and now you wanna go and punish me like that?" Ice protested. I should have known bringing his Domina up would have gotten his attention. He'd been more focused on his needs more than mine as of recently. "I'll do whatever it takes, baby."

He tried to get me revved up again, kissing on my neck and shoulders, which he knew always got me going, but my mind wasn't into it, which meant my body wouldn't betray me this time as it had done in years past whenever I was mad at him. After about five minutes of me not responding to his rushed advances, Ice finally stopped and lay on his side of the bed.

"You sure you didn't come?" He'd given up on trying to get me going, and sat up on his elbows, trying to figure out why his tried-and-true method hadn't produced the results he'd always gotten.

I shot him a look that turned him into a little boy. One of the things I loved about Ice was he didn't have to guess about anything, he reacted, and most times he was spot on. It was almost like Sin slowly turned him into a completely different man.

Part of me wondered if I was being selfish. After all, I enjoyed being an owned submissive, much like he enjoyed being on the right track to be owned by Sin. But, I hadn't changed my behavior around him. In fact, I couldn't remember when I felt more wanton, more sexual, with him, or anyone we played with, male or female. Even now, my body needed release. I wanted to slip into that blissful orgasmic sleep.

The house phone rang, and considering it was around 10 p.m., it could only have meant that Sin was calling. He sat up and got off the bed, answered the phone as he walked toward the bathroom.

"Yes, Ma'am, i'm here." His demeanor confirmed it was Sin, but he turned and walked back to me and gave me the phone instead, his shoulders slouched over. "Your Goddess wants to speak to you."

Ice's cell phone rang as he gave me the house phone, and he took his call in the sitting room, in enough earshot to be able to hear my call and deal with his at the same time. Hadn't he learned by now my Dominants don't discuss anything over the phone anymore, not after he was punished for breaking Sin's protocol some months ago?

"Good evening, my Goddess, what do You command of me?" I greeted her the way I always did when I first picked up a call from either her or Daddy, as House protocol dictated. I had become quite learned over the last couple of months, being able to switch between the submissive side of me and the regular everyday me to be able to deal with the rigors of my job and home life. I guess it's why I began to resent my husband. He hadn't made the transition yet, and I guessed in hindsight, I needed to try to be a little more understanding that this submissive side of him might be brand-new to him, whereas it was something I'd always known I would be dealing with.

"Good evening, My sajira, I hope that things are well tonight with you. I've missed My bitch." My Goddess was smooth over the phone tonight, almost sensually seductive. Usually she's all business when she's giving orders for the next day. "your Daddy and I have been talking about your next evolution, to make the process complete."

"What do You mean, Ma'am, and Your bitch really missed You, too," I purred over the phone, but I was confused. I had already considered myself owned by them, and they'd already changed my name when we were in Dubai, so I wasn't sure there were any more steps to take.

God, I *loved* it when she called me her bitch.

I was in for the shock of my life when she provided the answer to my confusion. "Baby girl, we are planning your collaring ceremony, to take place in around two weeks at the former Palace."

"my collaring ceremony, Ma'am?" I repeated the last thing she said. I still couldn't believe it! I had been reading on the online social networks that this was the next step, but I honestly didn't think it would have happened this soon. I'd only been with them for a little over six months, but then again, we'd known each other for years before my awakening.

"Are you ready to take this to the next level, sajira?" Neferterri asked. "your actions have told us you are, but I want to hear it from your mouth."

"Yes, Ma'am, i am ready. i'm in shock right now, to be honest, Ma'am," I answered, my hands still trembling. My heart raced furiously as I thought about the seriousness of what she told me. "i wasn't sure You wanted to take such a step for at least another six months or so."

I heard pieces of Ice's conversation with Sin, and from the sounds of it, he'd still had a few things to accomplish before she thought about taking the next step with him. Out of the corner of my eye, I could see him trying to strain to hear my conversation while trying to concentrate on his own affairs.

This bit of information I had no problems telling him. Besides, the rest of the community would hear about it soon enough, and I guess I wanted to rub it in, so when he was out with Sin, the other submissives would gush about the whole affair.

"There's one other thing I need, little one," I heard Neferterri say to me. "We will expect you to expand your circle of submissives to associate with, male or female. It doesn't matter to us, but you need some other experiences and points of view to draw from, as you won't be able to rely totally on us a hundred percent of the time for different things."

"Yes, Ma'am, i understand," I answered, and the first person who came to mind, I needed to get some information from either her or Ramesses to be able to begin on that task. "Ma'am, do You have any contact information for Scarlett? i would very much like to have her as my first within that circle."

Neferterri agreed. "As a matter of fact, I think it's safe to say that Scarlett will be an instrumental part of your growth as a sub-missive, baby girl. We trust no one else more to be a guide than her. Also, the name of the Palace is changing. you know how your Daddy is, He insists on making a splash for the spring."

I giggled at her remark. Daddy *loved* to make an impression.

"So, will i get a look at things before the ceremony, my Goddess?" I asked sweetly, hoping she would take the hint I really, really wanted to see the changes that had been made, so I could brag a little bit on the boards and at the munches.

She caught on really quick. "I actually wanted to talk to you about that. We'll discuss the specifics when Ramesses comes in from the DMV. Until then, be a good little girl and be patient; We promise it will be a profitable conversation to have."

As I hung up the phone, the possibilities of the conversation they wanted to have with me would surely drive me crazy for the next few days at least. She knew it would keep my attention.

I hated it when she teased me, but I couldn't get enough of her.

Ice hung up the phone, irritated after yet another berating conversation with his Domina. He was even more distressed by the look on my face. If I could have come from the mental stimulation and good news my Goddess had adorned me with, I would have screamed from the rooftops how good it felt to come that hard.

"I know you can't say anything about your phone call, so I won't ask what your Goddess said to you." Ice sulked, the remnants of his conversation still lingering in his body language.

"Oh, but this time I can." I nearly burst at the seams, ready to beat him over the head with the news. I sat up in bed, facing him with my eyes gleaming from the glow around me. He knew something big was about to be announced, but he had no idea. Finally, I screamed loud enough to cause him to clamp his hands over his ears. "I'm getting collared in two weeks!"

# FIVE ⚭ NEFERTERRI

"Yes, Sir, we'll be ready in two weeks; can you both make it?"

I don't know why He made me feel like a damn school girl when I talk to Him, but damn. I was hoping Amenhotep and paka would be able to make it here in time for the ceremony so much I felt like I was begging Him to confirm, so I could move on to an easier invitation.

"Yes, of course, My dear, we will definitely make the trip up for Your little one's collaring. I would be honored," He spoke over the phone. My relief couldn't be more evident in the quick squeal in my voice. He chuckled when He heard me. "I am glad I am only going to be a guest this time."

"Wonderful, Sir, I will email paka the packet that we are putting out. How are things otherwise? How is it down in the Islands?" I took the opportunity to be a bit more conversational. Ramesses was the more gregarious one, while I tended to observe and flow from the energy in the room. But I didn't always have His undivided attention, so I took the rare opportunity to enjoy Him.

"Well, it's quiet, and the sunsets are amazing. You and the kids should come down for a visit, give them somewhere fun to go outside of the country." He sounded so grandfatherly, the way He spoke about the girls. In a way, He was as much of a father to us as Ramesses' biological father.

"We would love to sometime over the summer, Sir," I responded to Him, dreaming about the killer suntan I would get under a sun that wouldn't be as covered with smog and haze the summers in Atlanta offered at times. "How is Your wife, by the way? I usually speak with her via email."

"she is doing beautifully, My dear. The new atmosphere has really taken a liking to her, and vice versa," He told me. I don't think He realized He was repeating what she had already told me a week ago, but I knew He didn't do email and technology too much.

"That is good to hear, Sir. I need to go see about the kids, since You mentioned it. I look forward to seeing You in a couple of weeks. I am anxious to see Your reaction to the additions to the house, and so is Ramesses."

"I am excited as well. I always wanted to do something like that, but sometimes you have to let the youngsters execute for you," Amenhotep answered. For a moment there, I could have sworn I imagined a slick grin spreading across Amenhotep's face. I guess the old man wasn't as slow of mind as He liked to lead people to believe. But then again, that's old school for you.

"I would assume Your Beloved has already started making the rounds to those on the master guest list concerning their respective attendance to the grand reopening?" Amenhotep asked.

"Yes, Sir, He's already out in Vegas speaking with Master Osiris and Lady Hatshepsut, and He should be flying out to Virginia tomorrow." The moment I said that, it brought a period of silence from Amenhotep.

"I see He's going ahead with the next phases in the plan," He finally responded.

I took a good look at the phone, and at that moment, I realized that the endeavor that my husband was about to undertake was a little larger than had been planned. "Amenhotep, are You telling Me Ramesses is out there trying to convince the Elders out there to expand?"

"That would be correct, My dear." He answered my question without hesitation. "You can blame Me for the slight misdirection. He is only executing the plan that we had in mind once He got over the shock of My no longer being in the Atlanta community."

He was right, I wanted to cuss him out, but I knew better. As I said before, Amenhotep acted a lot like a father to us both, and fathers tended to do things we might not initially like, but it always had a purpose and goal in mind. My husband always understood I, on the other hand, had my moments where I wanted to know it all, and then I would co-sign on it.

"Do not worry, My dear," He said, like He could read my thoughts. "This is His time to build upon His legacy within *Neb'net Maa'-kheru.*"

"Wait a minute, Sir." What in the bloody hell was He talking about? "I've never heard that name before in My life, Sir."

A slight chuckle escaped over the phone as I listened to Amenhotep explain to Me how much deeper things were about to become. *"Neb'net Maa'-kheru* is the Society, the Masters of Honor and Enlightenment, Neferterri," He began. "It is a gathering of honorable Masters within the national community who have developed a rather strong interpersonal network. Its ultimate purpose is to create a network of compounds for those within the community to converge in fellowship. My former *Palace* was the first of its kind. There were plans to build more, but I could not get two of the members to agree upon the locations of the next two compounds."

"Why was that?" I asked, trying to soak all of this in.

"Master Osiris and Master Seti are brothers both in Dominion and by blood. Fiercely competitive, about ten years back when the first expansion was conceived, they developed bad blood over a slave who chose to be with Osiris instead of Seti." He tried to give me a brief histoy, despite the fact that I didn't understand a word of it. "Ever since then, trying to get the two of them in the same room, much less on the phone to hash out their differences, has been futile."

"So, why is My husband out in Vegas trying to convince Master Osiris if His brother won't complete the circle?" I found myself enthralled as He provided more pieces to the puzzle. The plot thickened with each passing question.

"Osiris is the easier task because He is the one with the slave in question," Amenhotep explained. "It's Seti who will be the more difficult to convince. It would do Ramesses no good to tell Him that His brother is involved in the expansion plans again."

"You know My husband as well as I do, and He will try to be the mediator in this situation," I told Him. Ramesses could be stubborn like that. "Besides, perhaps with time, cooler heads can prevail in this attempt at the two of them reconciling?"

"I hold out hope that old wounds have healed. It has been a few years, after all," He stated. "What we old heads could not accomplish because of egos and tempers, perhaps Your husband can reforge, for the betterment of the Society."

"Tell Me more about this Society, Sir. Who are the other members?" I was curious, to say the least. "Will they be in attendance for the reopening?"

"Yes, paka is making the calls as we speak, My dear." Amenhotep's smile showed in His voice through the phone. "Lord Magnus, Seti, Osiris, and Me. Lord Magnus ascended at the end of the year; He is now Master Menes. Lady Hatshepsut is also a member, My dear. I also hold hope that You will soon be included within the

Society as well because, as You see, the Society was not meant to be exclusive to only the male Masters in this realm. There hasn't been a gathering this important in quite some time. The circumstances of this gathering are auspicious, to say the least. It will definitely be a night no one will forget for some time."

I understood where He was coming from, but I was still speechless. Things were about to be taken to another level, but at the same time, Ramesses and I were still parents, and we had to be careful not to forsake that responsibility. I'm sure my husband had already taken this into consideration, which was why the councils were being set up abroad, so he wouldn't think he was needed on a full-time basis away from home and Atlanta completely.

"I understand, Sir. I have a feeling I will need to talk to My husband while He is en route to the next destination. He will probably be in D.C. in the next couple of days to speak with Master Seti," I told Him. If anything, Ramesses needed to know this information, because I didn't think he had plans to tell Master Osiris he would be on the way to D.C. to see his brother.

"Well, My dear, I have a few more phone calls to make, now that I know Ramesses is setting the plans in motion," Amenhotep explained. "I look forward to seeing You and Your sajira, as well as to see how Your male submissive is coming along."

Yeah, I was looking forward to how my male submissive was coming along, too. In fact, I needed to find out for myself what he was truly capable of.

I heard a soft knock at the door, in a cadence I hadn't heard in at least three months. I walked to the door to open it, shocked by the surprise awaiting me a few seconds later.

It was a surprise I never saw coming…in ways I never imagined possible.

# SIX ☙ SAJIRA

"Damn, girl, what are you doing here? I wasn't expecting company today."

As part of fulfilling the tasks set out for me, I began to seek out different submissives within the community and elsewhere that I felt comfortable with and I could trust. I definitely agreed that I needed a larger circle to bounce ideas off and who could understand my frustrations if the need arose.

Scarlett was a no-brainer, and I had been texting back and forth with her when we weren't Skyping or talking on the phone or whatever. Having my Goddess' permission to keep in touch with her at will was a godsend, even though the majority of the time we were complaining about our respective husbands and the dumb shit they did more than submissive stuff.

paka was an easy choice, too, and thanks again to Skype, I could talk to her from my office at home. She took great interest in me while we were in Dubai for her wedding, and I thought it would be great to have her.

The personal visit I made to tiger was going to be a shock to his system, but I thought it would be the perfect change-of-pace perspective on submission that I would need to balance things out. That and it always helped to have a bisexual or gay male in your inner circle, especially when that male had boss makeup design skills and a flair for fashion. Mistress Sin always looked stunning and her makeup was flawless. Word around the community was that he was an excellent makeup artist and one of the better fashionistas in the A.

"Hey, baby, i hope you don't mind me coming through." I blew air kisses and gave him a hug as he let me into the house. It was especially brisk today, so I was relieved he didn't want to chat while we were at the door. "i wanted to chat with you about something, if you have a moment?"

"Sure, anything for you, boo." He took my coat and hung it in the foyer closet. We walked into the family room and took our seats on the couch, where he got comfortable in anticipation of a long conversation. "So, what's up, baby; what's on your mind?"

"Well, my Goddess thought it would be a good idea to expand my inner circle and She wanted to make sure i chose people i could trust. Would you be okay with being a part of that circle? i mean, you and Scarlett have always been close, from what she told me, and i know she would love it if we were closer friends, too."

I saw the smile spread across his face and I didn't have to guess what the answer was. "Girl, i was wondering when you would come to me! Of course i will!"

He hugged me so tight I thought he would choke me out. In the next moment, his body language changed. "Oh wait, so, what about your hubby; what would he think about this, boo?"

"i don't give a fuck what he thinks," I spat. "He's been on some other bullshit lately, so i'm not about to worry about that."

"Well, you might wanna change your tune once you find out what he's been doing while he's been training over here." tiger's facial expression turned to one of indifference as he studied my body language. "Mistress has been putting him through it, to say the least, not to mention the stuff he's been doing with me."

I narrowed my eyes, wondering about the cryptic nature of his statement. "And what the hell has he been doing with *you?*"

"Hold up, trick; ease back on the attitude, okay?" He held his hands up in mock protest. "He was with it, saying that he couldn't tell you about that side of him and shit, and i told him he needed to clear the air with you before he started exploring his bisexuality."

I blinked a few times, trying my best to process the last words he spoke. *Exploring his bisexuality?*

"i don't believe you, tiger; you can't be serious."

"i'm as serious as a heart attack, baby." He leaned back in his spot on the couch. "you can choose to believe me or not; doesn't make a difference to me, either way. But i have sucked his dick; i can tell you that much. In the interest of full disclosure, especially when you want me to be in your inner circle, baby, are you okay with me still being there? i love you like a sister, and i don't like hurting my sisters; Scarlett can vouch for that."

I didn't know what to think, but the signs were there, laid out on the table in front of me. He hadn't been able to get it up for a few weeks now, and he couldn't explain the reason why. Now, here's tiger giving me the smoking gun, and I still needed proof of the reason my husband hadn't been my husband since he declared his submission to Sin.

I had to appreciate his candor and honesty, even if the information was hard to take. He could have easily hid that from me, but it made it difficult to know which move was the right one to make. Was he after my husband, or was my husband beginning to do what was best for him?

"i still want you in my circle, tiger. i have no reason to believe you are out to hurt me, so i'm trusting you to be on my team, regardless of what you and your Domina are doing with my husband. Right now, my journey into submission is more important to me at this stage. i can't worry about what he's doing, and i don't want to know unless it becomes a threat to my marriage or my health. Are we clear?"

"Crystal clear, baby doll," tiger grinned, grabbing my hand to kiss the back of my palm. "Unless it goes against my Mistress' protocol, i'm with you. i love your Goddess to death, and She would kill me if i didn't assist in your growth."

I checked my watch and realized if I didn't go, I would be late for my visit with my Goddess. I kissed tiger on the cheek and got up to leave. "i appreciate what you've said, and i will keep it under advisement. i can't promise i won't confront him with the information you've given me, but i will be discreet with any other information we share."

"Look, sajira, if you were any other bitch, i wouldn't have said shit, real talk." tiger got up from his seat on the couch to escort me to the door. He grabbed my coat and helped me put it on, kissing me on the cheek. "your husband is a newbie, just like you, but the difference between you two is he's trying to fake the funk. i can tell you're in this for the long haul. Now, go and see your Goddess, darling, and give Her my best."

# SEVEN ⚮ RAMESSES

Reagan Washington National Airport, Arlington, Virginia…

I walked off the plane and made my way down to baggage claim to collect my luggage, already plotting in my head how I was going to deal with the task in front of me.

I walked by the limousine drivers and noticed a rather stacked and stout young lady, about six feet tall, maybe an inch short of that, holding a sign displaying my full legal name.

I was surprised to see her there to greet me, especially when I hadn't seen her before in my life. But it was a pleasant surprise to be escorted by such a lovely creature indeed.

I guess in hindsight I shouldn't have been too surprised, as I'd suspected Master Seti would spare no expense in making my stay in the DMV, as pleasant as he could. I'd called the day prior to my departure from Vegas to inform him of my arrival, as such was general protocol with any of the Elders associated with Amenhotep.

The driver was very attractive. Her distinct features put me in the mind of the Italian peninsula. She was clad in a pencil skirt, teasingly above the knee, and matching blazer, both black in color, and four-inch heels. Her lean, muscular frame left no doubt she could handle my luggage with little assistance from me, no matter how much my vanilla-centric chivalry wanted to oblige her.

"Good afternoon, m'Lord, my name is slave nadia. Please follow me to the car, Sir," nadia announced as she loaded the bags onto a cart and led me out to the parking lot. "Master has alerted me of Your presence, which is why i am driving You to the House, Sir. Master didn't want You to get lost. He informed me it has been a few years since You've been out this way."

I laughed at her statement. It hadn't been *that* long.

"Yes, slave nadia, your Master has a way of reminding Me of such things in the most grandiose fashion possible." We walked across the lot, and I was impressed to see the Cadillac Escalade Hybrid limousine we approached. "Very nice, slave nadia, your Master shouldn't have gone to all this trouble."

"Sir, if i am allowed to say so, He wanted to make sure You were especially comfortable while You stayed with us." nadia smiled, looking forward instead of turning back to make eye contact. "He doesn't make these accommodations for everyone, Sir, so it is an honor to be of such a special service to You."

I climbed into the backseat while nadia placed the luggage in the cargo area to prepare for the ride back to the estate. On the middle console was a *USA Today* newspaper, and packed in a cooler in the opposite seat from me was an assortment of soft drinks and juices and a bag of roasted peanuts.

"Master thought You would like a light snack before Your arrival, m'Lord." nadia read my mind before I could ask.

I smiled. This had sajira written all over this one. I would say shamise also had her hand in this, but there was no telling if she was at the house at the time nadia called to confirm the items sitting on the side of me.

"Remind Me to thank your Master upon our arrival, slave nadia," I responded as she slid into the front seat of the car. I noticed a slight blush spread across her face at my statement. That meant she knew she would be properly spanked for following her Master's protocol to the letter.

We made the trek, beginning from U.S. Route 1 heading toward I-395, passing through the intersecting streets that crisscrossed and made up the Alexandria area. I took a sip of the orange juice bottle by the time we crossed over I-395 and continued south heading toward Mount Vernon.

I was reading the paper as we passed by the shopping malls and department stores, going from the commercial into the residential area, when I felt eyes on me, trying to get a better look at what I was doing. I looked up and met a gorgeous pair of hazel eyes staring back at me with the intensity and heat of a desert sun. She lingered for a moment before those eyes softened and gave rise to a lust their owner wanted to act upon, but she wasn't quite sure if she should or not.

nadia tried to conceal her shy streak as she sneaked looks through the rearview mirror as she deftly moved through traffic. She tried to get a peek in right before the fork in the road would either take us to the estate or take us to the Mount Vernon estate, the home of our nation's first president.

We kept this dance up for another half-mile or so. Every time I caught her looking up at me, she giggled to herself and focused her eyes on the road again, trying to steal as many glances as she could before we arrived.

I purposely began staring at her through the rearview mirror. The next time our eyes locked, nadia found her fingers tracing the outline of the blazer. She nimbly lowered the mirror to an angle to where I could enjoy the view, and I noticed nadia had unbuttoned her blouse and revealed her bra. I licked my lips at the way the satin caressed her breasts.

She blushed at my open satisfaction at her exposure, keeping one hand on the steering wheel, using her peripheral vision to keep her eye on the road and on me at the same time, and taking her free hand to expose her right nipple for my further enjoyment. She moved the mirror back to a position to reconnect with my eyes, pouting her lips to blow kisses for a few fleeting moments.

By now, my manhood had made its presence very much aware to me, and I couldn't ignore what it obviously wanted my mouth to say. But this was neither the time nor the place to engage in that type of mischief, as it would be a direct violation of the rules of engagement, and my reasonable half understood that. However, my libido silently crept into the far reaches of where I kept the "Beast" at bay, beckoning to it, *I have the key to unlock your cage; all you have to do is beg for it.*

I wanted her to beg so badly it made me weak. I imagined her legs wrapped around the small of my back, growling in her ear as I took her in the backseat, the tint in the windows providing the perfect cover in broad daylight before finally getting on with completing the journey.

nadia sensed my dilemma, and I sensed she was in a bit of a quandary herself. The vehicle slowed for brief interludes, which alerted me to the intimation she was not yet ready to end this dance. Each pause at the stoplights was torture for the both of us, increasing the tension from a simmering boil into an ominous volcano that could blow at any moment

My intense stare into what I imagined were her now-bright green eyes let her know I was straddling the thin line between commanding her to pull the vehicle over to the first secreted location for a clandestine and ravenous merging of two bodies, and thinking better of it and commanding her to cover herself up before we arrived at the estate.

I shook off the lustful state I was in as best I could. I had further business to take care of, and I couldn't allow myself to let the "chairman of the board" fuck things up because it wanted to get wet for twenty minutes.

nadia slowed down long enough to make the turn to the street where the estate was located, stopping the vehicle long enough for the two of us to gather ourselves and for her to straighten her uniform to look presentable once we entered the compound. Once all was back in its place, nadia put the truck back in gear and we headed toward the house once again.

I didn't mind the cat-and-mouse games too much. In fact, it was a bit refreshing to see such a lovely woman nonverbally flirting without the pretenses of titles and station. Well, at least not entirely. The fact that I was a Dominant in this realm, and a Dominant nadia had developed a respect for, might have had something to do with her flirting on the edges. The way I saw it, she, in the brief time we'd shared the same space, developed a passion that was predicated upon her respect for my station, and the good things she had heard from her Master about me.

That was fine by me. It's not like I could not have had nadia hot and bothered under normal circumstances, but at the same time, it helped to not have had to put the litmus test out there.

The next time she looked up at me, I gave a wink, letting her know I wouldn't discuss this little interlude between us with her Master, and blew her a kiss from the backseat to consummate the brief dance between us.

nadia returned the gesture with a kiss in the mirror at me of her own, letting me know she enjoyed the dance as well, and a wink letting me know we could continue the dance again, with her Master's permission, whenever I was ready.

Sometimes, it's great to be Pharaoh.

# EIGHT ⚭ NEFERTERRI

"Good evening, my Goddess. i imagine You were not expecting me."

Those were the first words out of Scarlett's mouth as she presented herself, in her kneeling position, at the threshold of the front door of our new home.

The words out of my mouth would have been *oh my God*, but that would have been a gross misrepresentation of my feelings at that moment. It was a sight I honestly had no recent hopes of seeing: our precious shamise back amongst her family.

When Ramesses first told me he had heard from her while we were in Dubai, I honestly thought he was joking. When I realized he wasn't, my heart actually skipped a beat or two. Deep down, I believed she would find her way back within the House once again, but I tempered my hopes with a dose of reality as well. After all, she was on the West Coast now.

"Hi, baby. Yes, I will say I was not expecting you. I was actually awaiting sajira's arrival soon. she will be very happy to see you. Now, on your feet, My Scarlett," I commanded, pointing toward the loveseat in the living room for her to kneel near.

"Yes, my Goddess."

Once we settled to get a chance to talk a little more, I was dying to know what prompted the surprise visit, as she knew it was a breach of protocol to drop in unannounced.

Before our conversation could start, the doorbell rang again, alerting me to sajira's arrival. "Stay here, Scarlett. your sister is at the door."

I don't know who was smiling more at that moment: me, or Scarlett.

I opened the front door and allowed sajira to crawl to her place on the other side of the loveseat, where she was not aware of Scarlett's presence until she settled into her kneeling position and I commanded her to open her eyes.

"Oh my God, Scarlett!" she screamed, trying hard to fight back feelings to reach out and hug her. "i'm sorry, my Goddess, i didn't mean to—"

"It's alright, *this time*, sajira," I told her, stroking her hair and then tapping her on her shoulder to release from her position. "I was quite pleasantly surprised to see her as well."

"Thank You, Ma'am, it won't happen again," sajira sat on the floor opposite Scarlett. She was flustered from having been caught breaking protocol, and it showed. "i'm trying to figure out, well, that is to say—"

"Scarlett, your former sister is dying to know, what are you doing here?" I asked her, running my fingers through the familiar crimson-tinged tresses that once belonged to me. A similarly familiar purr escaped her lips, letting both sajira and me know she missed it as much as I did.

"Well, Ma'am, i'm not sure if You're going to believe this or not," Scarlett started, still enjoying the attention that I was giving her. "i'd guess i'd sum it all up in three words: i am divorced."

☥

*"Okay, spill it, baby. What the fuck happened?"*

This complete look of astonishment hit sajira and me, and I immediately commanded her out of her submissive mode. This was a conversation that Scarlett, Mercedes, and Kitana needed to have.

It was one of those rare times where the girls got to see me as something other than their Goddess, and it helped them balance a little bit sometimes. It helped me because we could have those times to be at ease around each other. Besides, I couldn't be "on" all the time. Maybe my Beloved could be, but he could afford to. They expected the "Great One" almost everywhere we went. He had his days where he turned it off, and no one could tell the difference except for me or the girls, but the expectation was always there.

We sat down on the couch while sajira walked into the kitchen to grab some Moscato and wine glasses. From Scarlett's body language, this had the makings of a very interesting story to tell.

"Well, once we got out to L.A., things were good for about a month." She took a sip of her wine as she recalled the events that led her to our doorstep. "A couple of weeks ago, this woman started calling the house, telling me she'd been sleeping with my husband since before we got married."

Scarlett didn't shed a tear as she recounted the events like they happened yesterday. In fact, I swore she couldn't suppress a grin and a giggle or two. I wasn't surprised. A polyamorous mindset could sometimes protect your heart in situations like this…sometimes.

"So, did you cuss her out? Did you confront her?" Kitana continued the barrage of questions.

"Well, considering I had plans at the beginning of the year to see my family and satisfy my service and kink fix, I really wasn't one to trip out about the whole affair," Scarlett explained. "So, I invited her over to talk about things."

"*You did what?!?!?*" Kitana protested.

"Relax sis, I didn't ambush her or fight her or anything," Scarlett told her. "In fact, once we got a chance to get to know each other a little better, things really started to take off between us."

Took off? Now, I knew my Scarlett had her moments where she could be a bit, well, altruistic, but befriending the "enemy" was not something I expected her to do, especially when the woman admitted she fucked her husband.

Something still wasn't adding up, though. If things were okay, why was she here?

"Okay, now you have me confused, baby," I interjected. "Why are you divorced, then? Sounds to me like she would be willing to keep the secret and have you both without the other knowing about it."

"Well." Scarlett grinned. "The reason I'm divorced is he had been in love with her the entire time. She felt I deserved to know. The wild part was the sex we had that night."

"Wait, what 'sex you had that night'?" I asked, trying to get a gauge on the situation. "You fucked her, baby?"

"Yes, I did, I couldn't help it, Goddess. She was sexy." Scarlett closed her eyes for a minute to take in the visual all over again.

"Damn, now I know it couldn't have been me, sis." sajira shook her head. "Ice would suffer; I can tell you that much. But something doesn't add up. Why do you look so sickeningly happy to be divorced?"

Scarlett, by this point, had the glow of a woman who had gotten away with murder. "I left one significant part out of the whole situation. The 'she' that I'm talking about…is a shemale."

"*What?!?!?*" we both screamed in unison.

"Yes. I couldn't turn down the opportunity; she was so damn sexy."

Scarlett reminisced as she continued to explain. "It was better sex than what I was having with my husband, that's for sure. I guess she was right. He isn't into biological women, never was. Being with me must have sealed the deal for him."

I kept fanning myself over the images in my head of Scarlett in various positions with the shemale her husband was sleeping with. The thoughts made me wetter than Niagara Falls. They both looked at me, no doubt sensing the sudden change in my demeanor. I couldn't help myself, and having them both there was not making things any easier.

Scarlett picked up on it, and she started to inch closer to me. "But that's not the most deviant part. I confronted him about the affair a few weeks later, and he basically confessed to his part in the affair. When I told him I knew about 'her,' he freaked out, offered to buy my silence and not tell his family or coworkers."

"I guess I should be mad at you since you got the chance to fuck a shemale before I did," I finally said, trying hard to recover from the heat covering my body. "I wonder if I need to punish you for that."

"Actually, Goddess, before You punish me, i have something to ask of You."

Scarlett switched to her submissive persona, changing the atmosphere in the room. sajira switched up on cue also and recovered back to her kneeling position.

"What do you request, My Scarlett?" I asked her, motioning her closer to me so I could hear her request better. "Or do I already have an idea of what you want to ask?"

Scarlett's eyes softened, casting her eyes downward, her silence giving rise to her apprehension to make the formal request. I already knew what she wanted, but I wanted her to say the words.

She wanted her name back.

"m'Lady, i am formally requesting to have my name restored within the House of Kemet-Ka. i have been suffering this entire time i have been here. To have You referring to me as anything other than the name that You and Daddy so lovingly gave to me has been torturous the last few months, and it's killing me right now." Scarlett finally uttered the words, a single tear falling down her cheek.

I would never admit it to either of the girls kneeling at my feet at that moment, but it was extremely touching to me to have Scarlett so lovingly ask, admitting to the torture she had self-inflicted since the separation. I imagined Ramesses sitting there, stone-faced, torturing her even more until he would *finally* say he would "think about it."

Knowing her Daddy didn't know she was even in the state, much less in the house talking with us, I felt I needed to inform my Beloved that our little one wanted to come back home.

"you do know that your Daddy is out of town at the moment?" I teased her some more, a soft giggle escaping my lips as I watched her tremble at the mere mention of Ramesses. sajira did the same thing with me, which was a trip at times. "I'll need to contact Him so He and I can give our final word. you know how your Daddy is."

"Yes, Goddess, i do." I detected a smile spreading across her face. She wanted me to be the first to give the word of her reacquisition. I felt it on her, and I returned her smile. "May i make the request personally?"

"Oh, I wouldn't dream of taking this conversation away from you, baby girl." I heard sajira trying to stifle a scream. She knew what was coming, and so did I.

She would soon be getting her sister submissive back.

But Ramesses was going to make her work to get her place back, and I had no idea once the phone rang as to what would happen next.

"Oh, before I do, there is something I need to discuss with the two of you first." I stopped before I completed the call. The phone conversation popped in my head from the other night with sajira. "I have a job offer for the two of you, but I will explain later, after we get this call out of the way."

I put the phone on speaker as he answered his cell phone. "Yes, darling?"

"Hi, Daddy, how are You doing?"

"Scarlett? What are you doing at My house? I wasn't expecting you for at least another week." Ramesses was genuinely surprised to hear her voice. That almost floored me. She really did surprise us all.

"It's a long story, Daddy; i'll let Goddess explain it to You later. i have a request to make of You." Scarlett's voice turned into a teenager in an instant.

sajira silently asked to move nearer to Scarlett, slipping behind her to rub her shoulders because she could feel the tension on her. I felt for her, too, but she was going to have to go through what her Daddy was going to put her through.

As though she were teleporting the thoughts to him, Ramesses commanded, "Make the request, Scarlett."

The bass in his voice froze sajira in her stance.

After a brief pause, Scarlett finally queried, "m'Lord, i am formally requesting to have my name restored within the House of Kemet-Ka, Sir. i have not been the same since being separated from You and my family, Sir. By Yours and m'Lady's command, i respectfully request to repledge myself to this House."

There was a long pause, which had Scarlett on her toes and sajira trying desperately not to break the silence. I sensed my husband's wheels turning in his head, trying to find a way to figure out how much Scarlett wanted her identity back.

For what we want most, sometimes there must be a cost that must be paid.

As quiet as it was kept, Ramesses had hurt for a few weeks after she finally left for good. He kept a public face when we had different things going on, and no one really knew the wiser. They simply assumed Scarlett was away on business. We never really even made it known she was no longer a part of the House because, in his heart of hearts, he was convinced she would be back with us. I never doubted she would come back to us for a moment.

After what probably felt like an eternity for Scarlett, Ramesses finally answered, "On one condition, little one."

"Name it, m'Lord," she answered without hesitation.

"In due time, My darling shamise. When the time is right, I will do exactly that."

# NINE ⚭ SAJIRA

"i'm sorry i left you, sis."

shamise and I were in the basement of our Owners' home, and she was helping me with the care of the leathers and the other equipment inside of Ramesses' and Neferterri's bags, showing me tricks she'd learned in her years in service to them. Neferterri had gone out to run errands while we took care of this task for them. There was nothing odd about leaving us in the House alone, as we'd all had keys anyway, in case one of the kids needed to be picked up and brought home from school early.

I had to admit the way she showed me some things made the process much smoother than what I thought I had been doing.

"It's okay, sis; the important thing is you're here with us now." I put down the leather paddle that I was cleaning to place a small kiss across her lips before resuming our duties. The truth was we'd never really lost contact, so it felt like she was on an extended rest or away on assignment for a job.

"i still feel like i let you down, sajira." She caressed my cheek after putting down one of the knives she was cleaning. "i was supposed to be helping you prepare for the way things are done within the House."

"Look, shamise, if i was in your position, i probably would have followed my heart, too." My mind went back to my husband and what decision might I have made if I were faced with the same choice.

"But that's the thing, sis," shamise contended, "i didn't think things through. If i'm honest with myself, i really didn't make the right decision. He led me to believe he could make me happy, and also let me come back here to be with you, Daddy and Goddess. The minute we touched down in California and got to the new place, i knew i'd made a mistake. He completely turned one-eighty on me."

I remembered the conversation Ramesses and Neferterri had had with me after shamise had been granted her "conditional release," as they termed it. They gave me permission to speak freely during that conversation, and I had to know why they didn't fight harder for her, make her stay with us because they knew her place was here.

Neferterri, who normally was the more emotional of the two of them, was absolutely pragmatic about the fact that sometimes things had to run their course before shamise would realize where her true place was and where she belonged. Ramesses, who usually was the more even-keeled and rarely showed his anger in public, admitted that it was a very emotional discussion, as he did not want her to leave, especially after nuru and jamii had left not a few weeks prior without too much of a word themselves. In the end, they said that they trusted shamise and that they knew her better than she knew herself. She would have a moment where she knew she'd erred big-time and would try to begin the process of returning to us.

Looking at how shamise was now as we were cleaning, I understood completely what they were talking about. It made me smile and gave me hope that perhaps, in time, they would come to understand me and read me as well as they did shamise.

"you have done a pretty good job keeping things up since i've been gone, sajira," shamise admitted after inspecting the leather floggers and carefully placing them back in the case. "How has your training been going?"

"It's been challenging, considering i don't know as much as you do, sis," I admitted, blushing a little bit over some of the things I'd gone through in the past few months. Some of it was deliciously embarrassing, and some of it was humbling, to say the least.

"Well, it's obvious that you have done well, baby. Daddy and Goddess don't simply bestow a name or a training collar on anyone." shamise grinned at me when she stated that.

"Knowing that, now i really am blushing." I was so flushed with embarrassment that I wanted to find a place to hide. I wasn't aware of the gravity of the situation until that moment. "i really wasn't sure what i was doing, and Goddess has a poker face that would make card sharks go batty. Not that Daddy is any easier to read, of course."

"That's their job, baby," shamise stated. "In time, you will be able to read them and be able to anticipate their wants, desires, needs, and the little things they sometimes don't always verbally communicate. Now that i'm back, the process will go a lot more smoothly."

That thought made me smile.

"So, tell me what else have you been up to?" shamise gave me the body language she wanted to vibe a little deeper into some things. "i've had a lot i've wanted to talk to you about, now that we're alone without our Owners present to overhear."

"Well, there's one thing i've been doing that has been helping with my slut training." I began blushing again, since it was the first time I'd even spoken to anyone else about the phone sex job. "i've been doing a side job doing phone sex for a company. It wasn't for extra money, but to get me to be comfortable with my sensuality."

"It's okay, sis; i had to go through the same process. It was some of the sexiest and sluttiest stuff that i'd done at the time," shamise told me. "It helped me deal with some of the vulgarity we deal with online and real time in the community."

"Yeah, you have a point there, sis." I nodded my head in agreement. Some of the stuff I'd endured whenever I was online would make a woman cringe sometimes. "i thought i heard a lot, but doing the phone sex opened up a new world of low-life crap."

"So, i would imagine you have picked up your share of fans, sis?" shamise giggled as she asked.

We'd finished repacking the equipment to House specifications and put it in its proper place in the private room in the basement. So, we found a spot on the sectional to lounge a bit before Nefer-terri returned from running errands to continue my training.

"Okay, sis, i've got to level with you. There is this one dude that has been calling on the semi-regular. i mean, he scares me, but he turns me on at the same time. Some of the fantasies that he has wanted to do have been on the edge a bit." I blushed as my face got hot with the shyness of a teenager.

"Like what, sajira?" shamise asked.

"Well, he's been having these fantasies of 'taking' me and raping me against my will." It took me a moment, but I finally came out and said it.

Rape fantasies…one of the most taboo subjects that can be brought up in BDSM, and I was having conflicting feelings it was making me hot.

shamise could see from my body language I was confused about my feelings. She put a hand on my shoulder and asked, "you, too?"

# TEN ⊗ NEFERTERRI

"Strip, Damian. Take off your clothes, all of them."

He hesitated a moment, already arousing my irritation.

I didn't have time for him to figure it out, but it was my fault for his hesitation. The last couple of times he'd visited, instead of training him, I ended up fucking his brains out. He'd end up naked by my command, and one look at his body and I got wet quicker than a blink of an eye.

Deep down, I wanted to believe he was submissive, but he was having a hard time accepting it. I think that might have been at the heart of my irritation with him, but it might have been at the heart of my irritation with myself. I hadn't given him the chance to serve me, instead of taking directives on how to please me. There was a difference between the two, and as much as we Dominas gave our male counterparts grief for thinking with the "other head," I was proving no more immune to my urges because of a man who towered over me when he was allowed to be on his feet.

Today, I was going to find out whether or not the problem lay with him, or with me.

"Goddess?" Damian's hesitation to act on my commands bordered on the criminal. Instead of taking the berating approach, I thought back to previous conversations, to see if I could use them to get through to his submissive mind.

During our conversations about his submission, he had told me when he questioned his desires to submit to women at times, how every time he went out in public as a submissive male, he would be misunderstood by other submissive males who were all too willing to be fuck toys for any Domina willing to have them, and why he wanted to kneel to me so badly. Yes, there was one hell of a mutual attraction, but once the sex was over and the conversations faded, the service aspect had to be there. Ramesses and I demanded it of the girls; there was no way I could get away with having him boiled down to being nothing more than the fuck toys he didn't want to emulate.

"you said you wanted to kneel at My feet, to serve Me and to serve your Sir, how you didn't want to be used and fucked like a rag doll by your Domina." My voice and my face were stern as he kept his eyes downward, absorbing the words being spoken in his direction. "Was that all lip service to seduce Me into keeping you?"

"Goddess, may i speak freely?" Damian asked.

"you may speak freely, Damian."

I sensed he wanted to obey my command. His body trembled, letting me know of his inclination to obey, but his mind and body were at war with each other, trying to figure out which would have the upper hand.

"Thank You, Goddess." With his eyes focused on the space in front of him, he tried to find the words to express his feelings. "As much as i want to serve You, i barely know You. Every time we try to have a conversation before we fall into protocol, we end up fucking like rabbits. i want to be able to serve You, but i need to know how to serve You. Does that make sense?"

His response hit me like I'd been shocked with electricity. For the first time in years, I was at a loss for words. The last time I'd even thought to have a meaningful conversation with a male submissive was when I was helping Sin with tiger years ago. I realized maybe I was the one out of practice, and I needed to step up my game to make sure I was the Domina I knew I was.

He didn't need to know I was off-balance, though.

"you are right, Damian; we have been a little hot and heavy for the past few months," I acknowledged. I wasn't about to let him off the hook, either. "However, the conversations we have had, you hadn't inquired what it might take to serve Me, either. And don't think for a minute I held a gun to your head while you pleased Me, Damian…and for the record, you have pleased Me *very* well."

A smile crept from his lips with my last statement before dissipating as quickly as it appeared. *Good boi*, I thought to myself, *you're learning more than you've let on.*

"In order to learn what pleases Me without involving sexing Me, I propose we start today by figuring out what you've learned from our conversations about what pleases Me." I wanted to find out how much he'd paid attention while he was busy dishing out information. "What pleases Me, Damian?"

Sitting back in the lounger in his living room, I watched his facial expressions change from confidence to uncertainty and back to confidence again. I watched his body, still clad in the muscle shirt and shorts he'd greeted me in when I'd first arrived, and my body and mind had waged their own war of which would win out based on the visual stimuli my eyes feasted upon.

My mind was intent on winning this battle, but my body put up a damn good fight.

"It pleases You when i'm able to serve You at Your whim, Goddess." He started to recount some of the conversations we'd had in the beginning. "It pleases You when i am able to provide a foot massage when You've had a long day at work. It pleases You when i have learned other skills to enhance my service to You, such as my ability to know how You like Your coffee, Your herbal tea. And i learned how to make a Tiramisu a couple of days ago, if it would please You to try it?"

If he wanted to endear me to him, he'd said the magic word! He'd proved he'd paid attention by learning the recipe based on a conversation we'd had a month ago where I happened to mention

Tiramisu as one of my guilty pleasures, but I never found anyone who could make it properly without having one of the girls heading over to Maggiano's to get it.

I tried to keep my enthusiasm under control, but inside, I was squealing because he was meeting my expectations in such a short time. Hopefully, in time, he would exceed them.

"Yes, it would please Me very much to try your Tiramisu, Damian."

He asked for permission to get the dessert. Upon my nod, he walked into the kitchen to grab the dessert, making sure he didn't waste the saucer he'd placed it on.

It took everything within me to keep from raping him on the spot again as he walked toward me with the saucer in his hands, slowly falling to his knees without spilling the saucer, and taking the fork in his hand, cutting a piece of the Tiramisu and offering it to me. "If it pleases You, my Goddess, would You take a bite and tell me if You like it?"

I nodded as he lifted the forkful of the dessert to my lips. I opened my mouth to take in the morsel, and, to put it not-so-delicately, the explosion in my mouth was orgasmic! Every bit of flavor in that small piece was enough to make me want to squeeze my legs together to keep from coming.

The smile on his face only enhanced the experience for me. He'd not only gotten the recipe right, but he'd put something more into the recipe. I just knew it! "Oh my God, boi, you put some serious skills into that!"

"i'm happy You liked it, Goddess." He blushed as he continued to feed the rest of the slice to me. "It took a few tries to get it right, and thankfully, it came out right before I spent too much more money trying."

I was honored by the effort. This was the type of effort in service I wanted him to understand and learn, and it only took us to keep from ravaging each other to find out what he could do.

I had a few more questions he needed to answer before anything more happened today. "Do you understand the rules of the House, pet?"

"Yes, Goddess," he answered. "i must obey You and my Sir."

"Yes, pet, you must always obey." I took the last bite of the dessert he fed me, enjoying it and the delectable piece of property that would soon belong to me. "you must always obey, baby boi, no matter what I or your Sir ask of you."

"i understand, my Goddess." He moved to take the saucer into the kitchen, shifting his body to face me to ask permission to leave my presence, when I placed my fingers over his lips.

"There's one more thing I want you to do, Damian."

"Yes, Goddess, it's my pleasure to serve You."

"Good, because I want you to fuck Me…now."

# ELEVEN ⚬ SHAMISE

"What do you mean, 'you too'?"

sajira gave me a look that could have cut through glass.

The look on my face let her know this was going to be a rather long conversation between sister slaves.

Since we were already finished with the cleaning duties we were tasked with before Neferterri was due back to the house, we got more comfortable on the sectional so we could bare souls.

"Okay, sajira, i'm gonna level with you," I began, trying to find the courage to explain myself. "i have been having the same type of rape fantasies you have been having. i didn't know how to bring it up until you admitted about what your Uber-Dom was up to, and, well, here we are."

sajira slid closer to me on the couch, touching my hand as she stared into my eyes, trying to find something that would let her know this was a cruel joke I was playing on her.

A few moments later, those same eyes she stared into gave her all she needed to know.

"i really didn't know who to tell, sis, honestly," sajira confided, her eyes misting. "i eventually want to tell Daddy and Goddess, but i really wasn't sure what their reaction would be to it."

Being the more experienced submissive, although I will admit my mindset is more slave-like than submissive now, I felt my sister submissive needed to be brought up to speed on our Dominants. If anything, it would help settle her mind a little bit and not be so fearful of them being judgmental. I felt like she did a few years ago, when I finally admitted I wanted more intense public play, edgier play.

"sis, Daddy and Goddess do care very deeply for us; you do know that, right?" I waited for her reply.

I got a hesitant nod from sajira; her little girl persona going into full mode. I brought her to me, stroking her hair, feeling her body finally stop trembling.

"The Dominants that you have the pleasure and the honor to submit to have been around for a long time, sis," I quietly told her, stroking her cheek. "you and i both know there are few like them in the community, and i have been in this community longer than you, even though you knew them from the swing side of things."

"Yes, i know, shamise." sajira nodded. "Every time i'm on the online boards and i sign off with the House name, i get hit up by email from other submissives trying to find out how i'm able to do it."

I laughed at her last comment. That question had been around as long as the House had been in existence. Even in poly circles, they couldn't figure out how the submissives of the House are able to serve "two Masters."

"That's okay, it's not their business how we do what we do, sajira," I retorted, kissing her cheek. "All you need to know is that as long as you focus on your place and your responsibilities to them, both as individuals and as a cohesive unit, then you will be fine."

I'd had this same conversation with jamii and nuru, too. Whenever I talked with them, it felt like I had to constantly reassure them of their place in the House, which was how they ended up doing the stupid nonsense they did in leaving, but this felt different. sajira was already friends with Daddy and Goddess before she'd made the transition over to the dark side.

I'll admit that it was tiresome to have to do that, and I had no intentions of repeating it again. I like her too much to have her go through those feelings when they weren't necessary.

"Do you want for us to request a free speech period? we do have that right within the House," I suggested, trying to comfort her a little. The free speech period gave us the opportunity to speak to our Dominants without fear of repercussions or the idea that we're "topping from the bottom."

"Yes, sis, i would like that very much," she answered, feeling a lot better about things now. "That would definitely help me, especially having you there."

"No problem, sajira." I needed her, too, craving the connection more than I realized. "Now i need to worry about where i'm going to live, now that i'm back in the city."

sajira perked up on me almost as soon as I finished my pondering aloud. "you are staying with me, no exceptions, at least until you get your own place set up."

My eyebrow rose quickly, which caused sajira to giggle uncontrollably. "i was just saying, sis. you need to be somewhere close to the House, and i want you there with me. What do you say?"

It was a tempting offer, but I had to wonder why she'd made the offer without talking to her husband. After all, it's his house, too.

"sis, don't you think you need to speak to your husband about taking me in?" My warning flags went up; she'd made the offer too quickly. "Is there something i need to be aware of?"

"Well, shamise, to be honest," she began, her body language

changing. "Things at home are tense right now. Ice has changed ever since he began to take his training seriously with his Domina. i was thinking maybe we could help him balance out, because he's not the same man i married."

I was afraid she was going to say that.

I wasn't sure if I wanted to be in the midst of another power struggle or not. I'd left one out in L.A. and that had left me drained mentally and physically. Yeah, sure, I'd had fun while going through it, but once the adrenaline rush was over, it really had become a chore to keep up the mess.

But, I did need a place to stay, and being with my sis would be good for us both. It would give us more time together to bond and have a little fun as well. I mean, I was a newly divorced millionaire now.

"Okay, sis, i'll stay with you." I reluctantly accepted her offer. "It should be an interesting time, to say the least."

"There is something else i wanted to talk to you about." sajira's eyes softened and her shoulders slumped like she was resigned to tell me what was on her mind, whether she wanted to or not. "i talked to tiger a few days ago about helping with my journey into submission and serving Daddy and Goddess, and he said he would, but—"

"But, what, sis?"

"he said that he and Ice had been intimate, like recently," she answered, trying her best to keep the tears from falling. "i told him that i didn't care about what he did, but the truth is, i do care. he's still my husband, despite the bullshit he's been doing ever since he began training with Sin."

The protective mode inside of me kicked in big-time. I wanted to strangle tiger, but knowing him, he did what he felt he needed to do, and he believed in full disclosure. We'd always been like that, so it didn't surprise me that he would do the same with sajira. "Do you want Goddess to talk to Sin and get Her to redirect his focus? She's not going to be happy about what he's been doing."

"i don't know anymore, sis; this is getting more complicated by the day." sajira wasn't sure if telling Sin would make matters better or worse, and I could understand why. Sin was a very strict disciplinarian, and any information that she got when it came to the submissives under her charge behaving badly, she took the punishment to the extreme. The last time tiger was punished for a transgression, he was in chaste for six months. While tiger had the discipline to deal with that type of punishment, Ice was new, and something like that would break him. "he hasn't even fucked me the way he usually does in months. If it weren't for the attention that Daddy gives me—"

"Calm down, sis." I put her head against my chest, consoling her as much as I could. She was at her breaking point, not only in her marriage with Ice, but with her service to the House. I felt it on her, and it felt like she wanted to give it all up to have her marriage back the way it used to be. The problem was, she couldn't go back. None of us could. "If what tiger says is true, i'll have a chat with Ice to see if I can get his head screwed on right."

She looked up at me, her eyes pleading with me not to intervene, but my mind was made up. She wiped the tears from her eyes and straightened up, almost like she wanted to make her own stand. "No, sis, he's my husband; i can't have you or anyone else fighting my battles for me. What type of submissive would i be if i can't handle something as simple as getting my husband in line? i'm expected to handle my affairs, whatever they may be, unless it gets to the point to where i might need help, and that's what i plan to do. i wouldn't be a good fit for the House, and considering i'm getting collared, that is not something i want on my conscience."

I kissed her lips gently, smiling at the decision she'd made. Yes, I still wanted to protect her because she's family, but she was right, she had to work this out on her own. "That's my girl; i'm proud of you."

"Don't pat me on the back yet, sis." sajira smiled. "i still have to take care of business, and he needs to man up or step aside. If he doesn't, then i guess this marriage is over."

# TWELVE ✿ RAMESSES

Master Seti's home was a cozy ranch, if you can call a six-bedroom home cozy.

Perfectly landscaped lawn and garden in the front yard, no doubt the work of one of his slaves. A tree line surrounded the house, both thick enough and tall enough to keep the neighbors from getting a look at the girls either sunbathing or anything else they might be engaged in.

Considering he was in a beautifully sculpted and historic neighborhood that spawned a lot of activity, Master Seti enjoyed a good deal of insulation and isolation, and that was saying a lot in terms of the privacy I observed.

nadia pulled into the driveway and moved the car around to the rear of the house, parking the vehicle at the end of the row of five cars that were lined up in their particular spaces. Master Seti was always a stickler for uniformity.

As she unloaded my luggage from the SUV, another of Seti's girls arrived, immediately kneeling at my feet to announce her presence to me.

"Good afternoon, m'Lord; my name is slave amirah," she told me, taking my hand and kissing the back of my palm. "If You will be so kind to follow me, Sir, i will escort You to Master."

amirah was damn near a carbon copy of nadia in physical stature, except she displayed softer curves and what looked to me as an Arabic heritage. She was adorned in a short sundress and heeled sandals, which was nice to see in the early summer weather, but her attire would be shed once we got back inside the house. It was Seti's protocol that his girls wear absolutely nothing while within the walls of the house.

We walked through the back sunroom, passing through the kitchen, where I noticed Seti's service slaves preparing dinner for the evening before turning the corner into the throne room. Seti sat in his chair, talking on the phone with someone when we entered.

amirah assumed her kneeling position and waited silently until Seti finished his conversation. He acknowledged our presence in the room and quickly finished his conversation.

"Master, i present Lord Ramesses, Sir." amirah settled into her kneeling position as she spoke; her eyes still cast downward.

"Thank you, slave amirah; you may join your sister in unpacking Lord Ramesses' bags in the bedroom," Seti commanded.

"Yes, Master. Thank You, Master," amirah replied before getting to her feet and disappearing from the room.

"Welcome, Ramesses, I trust that Your trip was safe?" Seti asked me. "Please, sit down. I trust nadia made sure You were comfortable on the trip home."

"Yes, Sir, the trip was safe, and nadia made sure everything was attended to in a proper manner." I insisted on keeping my poker face obvious, not wanting to give myself away. Seti had a habit of reading body language in the past, so I prepared against his attempt to study me to find something that might spawn a question I had no intention of answering.

"Good, considering she volunteered to pick You up from the airport, I wasn't sure if she would have broken protocol because of her affinity for You," Seti admitted, which caused a small smile from me, but not wide enough to give myself away. "Now, to business, youngster, I understand You have been putting together some rather aggressive plans down in Atlanta. What brings You here?"

"Well, Master Seti, I would like to duplicate the plans I have for NEBU in Atlanta here in the DMV." I explained the first part of my proposal, studying his body language. He seemed intrigued by what I had to present. "I have the plans for three such compounds in the initial plans, with expansion plans if the first three become viable."

"Okay, where did You have in mind for the compound You are proposing here, Ramesses?" Seti leaned forward in his chair as he inquired. "I'm assuming You're not trying to have the compound in Maryland, I hope?"

I pulled an aerial of the location I'd had in mind, showing a 300-acre tract about an hour away from his home. "I was looking at Fredericksburg, Sir. If we can get things implemented within the month, we can be up and running within six months. It's secluded, completely away from everyone and everything, which makes it a perfect location to be self-sufficient."

I studied Seti's face to gauge his thoughts, but he gave no clues as to whether he thought it was a good idea or not. He kept looking over the property, its location and reference point to I-95, as if his wheels were turning in overdrive.

Finally, after what seemed like a few hours of waiting for me, but what only amounted to a few minutes, Seti finally said, "All right, I think it's possible, but I don't think that it can be executed in the time frame You are thinking it can be done."

"I beg to differ, Sir," I protested, expecting this particular argument. "The business plan is solid, and I have already gotten confirmation from the Elders in Vegas. The plans are a go out there and should be coming to fruition before the Christmas holidays, in time to begin operations in the New Year."

"Ramesses, this ain't Vegas. Those jokers out there seem to think they can do anything they please without at least stopping to think about things," Seti countered, obviously not thrilled I had mentioned the Vegas contingent because of one person in particular.

Master Osiris.

Seti and Osiris were blood-related, and Osiris was Seti's older brother.

The disdain Seti showed for the Las Vegas BDSM community stemmed back from a personal grudge and old wounds that had yet to be healed from nearly a decade ago. Those wounds included a certain slave who served Master Osiris to this day, slave keket.

"Master Seti, if You would like confirmation, You are welcome to speak with Lady Hatshepsut, with whom You have no grudge to bear against Her," I compromised with him. "I assure You, this is legit, and not some scheme to something else You may have in Your mind. As long as You have known Me, have I ever led anyone with false pretenses?"

That direct question seemed to calm him down for the moment. In the next moment, he was on the phone with Lady Hatshepsut, having a very intense speaker phone conversation regarding the *Temples of Deshret* project.

Once the pleasantries were out of the way, I listened intently as Seti began his assault, trying to find as many roadblocks as could be had. Each one was met with a resounding "that's already been taken care of, Seti" coming from the other end of the conversation.

Finally, after all of the concerns and roadblocks had been abated, Seti and Hatshepsut spoke their farewells, with a special goodbye for me, with the confirmation both she and her boi would be coming down to Atlanta for sajira's collaring.

Seti stared me down the minute the call ended.

He forgot I wasn't as young as I once was, and that stare-down didn't work on me anymore.

His glare was returned by one of my own, and while the respect was still there, it was accompanied by an intensity that let him know I was a force to be reckoned with, and things had changed in the last ten years since I was last in his presence.

This time, I was well prepared for the confrontation.

Earlier in my journey, I will admit, I was in awe of Master Seti. Sure, I'd been active in the scene in Atlanta for a long time with Amenhotep, but I had rarely ventured outside of the state much, except for business purposes, which left very little room to attend the scenes when I ventured into Chicago, L.A., Philadelphia, or any of the other cities my business took me to.

The first time I came to Virginia with Amenhotep to meet Seti, I was on edge, scared to say the wrong thing to him during our interactions. After all, I was a rookie for the most part, and I was still trying to keep from embarrassing my mentor.

Not anymore.

The guard was changing.

His body language changed, relenting to the fact he would not be getting his way this time. A smile spread across his face, and he extended his hand toward me.

"So, what did You have in mind for this particular location, Sir?" Seti asked me without another shred of disgust or contempt in his voice. "I want all of the details to take to the persons I know will make this work in this part of the country better than on the West Coast."

From there, for the next six hours, we hashed out the same details, with some changes Seti wanted different from *Deshret*, which I suspected he wanted mainly to keep from copying his brother completely.

All that was needed was a name.

After the discourse we'd just gone through, I didn't dare try to presume anything else, and I wanted this to continue as smoothly as possible.

"Do You have any ideas, Sir?" I asked, more feeling the effects of the jet lag than anything. My creative juices were completely shot, although I had jotted a few ideas down, but I saved this conversation for a strategic purpose, to stroke his ego.

I waited for his wheels to grind a bit, and Seti didn't disappoint, taking his index finger and stroking it along the side of his temple.

Out of the blue, the name of the compound seemed to come to him. "Thebes."

This, of course, is in correlation to the former capital city of ancient Egypt. It was a fitting parallel, considering the location of the compound was near the U.S. capital.

"I believe that will work, Sir," I concurred with the name choice.

"You think so, Ramesses?"

"Master Seti, I couldn't have come up with a better name for this particular location, and I am honored You would be involved with this endeavor. I thank You, and Master Amenhotep thanks You as well."

"Speaking of Amenhotep, I suspect He will be in attendance to the collaring ceremony?" he queried.

"Yes, Sir, Neferterri has probably gotten in touch with Him to make Him aware. If I know Him, He will be back in Atlanta in a couple weeks," I answered. "Would You and the girls like to attend, Sir?"

"Consider it an honor, Ramesses," Seti responded after taking my extended hand back to him to shake.

nadia entered the room and assumed her kneeling position near her Master's presence. "Master, dinner is ready, Master."

I tried to take my eyes off nadia, but she looked better without clothing than with the outfit she'd had on escorting me to the limousine.

Seti noticed this, and without missing a beat, commanded, "slave nadia, you may escort our guest to the dining room, as reward for following protocol in escorting Him home."

nadia nodded, adjusting her position toward me. "It would be my honor to escort You to Your place in the dining room, m'Lord. If it pleases You, i can prepare the plate for You also."

"Thank you, My dear, and thank You, Sir, for Your accepting the proposal." nadia took my arm to lead me to the dining area. "I believe that You won't be disappointed with the end result and the possibilities."

# THIRTEEN ⚇ SAJIRA

"I'm home, baby."

I stepped through the door, shouting throughout the house. shamise was a step behind me, taking the surroundings in for a bit.

We started in the kitchen in search of my husband, then moving to the living room, following the faint noises coming from the basement of our home. Considering it was the midst of basketball season, the "man cave" became the logical spot Ice would be.

I blew out some air. In passing the kitchen, I saw the dishes hadn't been done, which meant he had been down there the entire day. It irritated me to no end. I didn't ask much of him on his off-days except some minor chores around the house, and he'd been increasingly neglecting those chores the past few weeks.

That was about to come to an abrupt halt.

As we walked downstairs, the smell of hot wings and beer filled my nostrils, and I could hear the sounds of the commentators coming into audible focus. I could nearly predict what I was about to see when we finally found him.

Sure enough, lying in his recliner, passed out and smelling of Coronas, was Ice. He wasn't quite snoring, but from the sounds I knew all too well, he was about twenty minutes from reaching that pitch.

I shook him awake, the frustration evident in my voice. "Ice, wake up. I need to talk to you."

He woke up with a start, trying hard to focus his eyes on the source of his sudden abrupt awakening. "What the…oh, it's you. I thought you were out with your *family*."

shamise sized up my husband, regarding his demeanor before she greeted him. "It's good to see you, too, Ice. It's been a long time, hasn't it?" I could tell she was trying to diffuse the tension building between us.

"It's damn good to see *you*, Scarlett. So, when you gonna stick around for good? I thought you were out in L.A. with your *husband?* I can't believe Kane let you marry that punk ass." Ice was slurring all over his words, which added to my embarrassment.

"I thought you were supposed to be cleaning up the house while I was gone?" I asked him, trying to avoid the stench on his breath from the beer.

"Well, I didn't feel like it at the time," Ice gruffly answered, glancing sideways at shamise and giving a sly smile. For a minute, I felt like he was trying to show out for her benefit, and I was not about to have that.

I composed myself a bit. I was not about to have this get ugly, especially when I wanted shamise to stay with us. The last thing I needed was to see the tension and decide she really didn't want to be caught up in some madness.

Ice kept it up. "So, what are you doing here anyway? I thought you weren't going to be home for at least another few hours because you had some tasks to complete or whatnot?"

"We got done with our tasks early, and I need to ask you something," I knew he wasn't in the right frame of mind to hear this, but at that point I really didn't care. "shamise is back in town, but she's needing a place to stay until she closes on the house she's buying in a month or two. I was thinking she could stay here with us; would that be all right?"

Now, let me tell you something about Ice: He was very territorial when it came to the house. Friends and family didn't do overnight stays because he was difficult to deal with and because of the rules he expected people to abide by while in "his house." Our nieces and nephews hated staying with Uncle Ice as the rules were too strict

So, imagine my complete surprise when my husband looked shamise up and down like she was the next dessert after dinner was over and said without hesitation, "Sure, she's welcome to stay as long as she needs to. Mistress always says we should help our own whenever we can."

I reached my boiling point.

"What the fuck?" I completely lost it. "So you mean to tell me all these damn years you've been giving people…not people, family… grief about staying one night here, and because your *Mistress* said so, now all of a sudden, we're the goddamn Holiday Inn?"

Ice didn't bat an eyelash, and I noticed he wasn't as drunk as he was before. I didn't know if that was going to worry me or anger me more. "I don't think you heard me, woman. If shamise wants to stay, she's welcome to stay for as long as she wants."

I felt my hand ball into a fist; he had one more snap remark to make before he found himself holding his jaw on the couch. I met his eyes, coming within breathing space of where he stood, daring him to say something else.

A hand across my shoulder slowed me down.

"sajira…sajira, let it go, sis," I heard shamise calling from behind me, and I felt her presence surround me. "He's a little lit right now, but we have the answer you wanted, so, help me with the bags in the car, please?"

I poked Ice in the chest with my fingers a few times before I told him, "You better be lucky she was here to keep me sane, Ice. I can't believe what's gotten into you lately."

"Naw, baby, I see things much more clearly than I have in a long time," Ice shot back, taking another swig of his Corona. "Some things will be changing around here soon; I can promise you that."

☥

It took me a few hours to calm down, but having my sis there helped tremendously.

The claps of thunder and the exquisite sounds of a passion storm kept shamise and me company as we wound down from a productive day.

"i swear, his Mistress is gonna be the death of him," I mused out loud. I didn't want to drudge it back up because the flow was so mellow, but I had to get it off my chest.

"Stop worrying about it, sis; you're going to ruin my buzz from this wine," I heard shamise reply.

We were sitting in one of the guest bedrooms, which had now become her semi-permanent home. She lay across one of the love seats in the bedroom while I sprawled across the Goddess-size bed in the middle of the room. We were enjoying glasses of a bottle of Vernaccia di San Gimignano wine, which was a gift from Ramesses and Neferterri for my birthday a couple of months ago.

God, I loved it when they spoiled me, and I spoiled them, too.

We were getting rather tipsy and really, really cozy and comfortable with each other, especially after Ice had finally crashed on the couch for the night. So, it gave us some time to actually do some real girl talk amongst ourselves, without our Dominants sneaking a peek or eavesdropping on the conversation.

"i forgot how spoiled rotten we are," shamise said as she continued to sip from her glass.

"It's one of the things i love most about them. i read it on the boards online about how some of the other girls are pissed their Dominants hardly acknowledge much of anything."

"Yeah, sis, they do have a way to definitely make you want to please them, especially when you get to enjoy some of the finer comforts of the House." I poured another glass.

We were both naked underneath the robes that we wore, and I stole looks at shamise's body while we were giggling our heads off. Her legs were to die for, with her being nearly six feet tall and all. We're both thick girls, and I had the more ample hips and thighs, but she had the ass to match, and her breasts were more than a handful. Considering that Daddy had large hands, that's saying a lot.

Not that our Dominants cared either way, though. We both get used, and used quite well now that I thought about it, and I wouldn't have it any other way.

From head to toe, I lusted and blushed at the things I wanted to do to her on her first night here at the house. Technically, we never got a chance to "consummate" the sisterly bond between us, which was something I fantasized about the entire time she'd been gone from us. I wanted to taste her, I wanted her to taste me, and it was getting me extremely moist having the thoughts that invaded my mind.

The wine didn't hurt matters, either.

The storm outside amplified the storm stirring from within the depths of my sex, and I was ready to immerse myself inside of the nasty images of our bodies melding together in our own private passion. In fact, the nastier the thoughts I had became, the warmer my body felt with each passing second.

"i really want you, shamise." I heard the words flow so freely from my lips that it nearly scared me. "i can feel my pussy throbbing at the thought of tasting you."

shamise didn't bat an eyelash. She slid off the love seat and slowly made her way over to where I was on the bed. The wine had her balance a little off, so she resorted to crawling across the carpet and meeting me at the foot of the bed.

"Kiss me, sajira," she whispered.

Our lips met, our tongues began to mingle and explore for the first time since she'd asked to be a part of the House again. The shivers the kiss sent across my clit were indescribable. My nerves were on edge, and I could feel every waft of her breath on my skin.

My own breathing became shallow, as my mind tried to realize what I had visualized all those months was actually coming to a climactic conclusion. This was no longer a dream, and the ever-building tsunami present between my thighs was clear and indisputable proof of that reality.

shamise broke our kiss, letting her hands roam from my breasts to my hips, opening my robe to get a better look at my body. I shivered at the thought of what could have been going through her mind as she tasted my nipples, running them between her teeth. I could feel the sweet stinging as she bit them hard enough to make me moan at the sensation.

I readjusted my position at the edge of the bed, spreading my legs to welcome her between them. shamise wrapped her arms around the small of my back, which only made me succumb more to the scene between us. She kissed me once more, slightly grabbing my hair as her tongue probed my mouth deeper this time, sealing our mouths to where it seemed like she was taking my breath away. I heard her moans through our embrace, feeling her nails raking down my back as the kiss continued.

"i've been wanting to do this ever since i came home," she whispered after breaking our kiss again. "i needed this, and i know you've been dreaming about me, too."

God, I hated when I was so transparent.

"i want you, too, baby," I answered with slight tears in my eyes. "you have no idea how badly i wanted this to happen."

The smirk that spread across her face let me know I didn't have to say anything. My body had already told her everything she wanted to hear.

She pushed against my chest, laying me down on top of the comforter. Feeling the plush fabric only enhanced the silky-smooth sensations flowing through me, and once her tongue began to explore my clit, if I could have melted like warm butter, I would have at that very moment.

"Ohhh my God, baby, that's it." I pulled shamise to invade my sex. "i want you to, please, take it."

"you taste so good, sis, mmmm," shamise uttered as she took her time tasting me, savoring me as much as she savored the wine we were drinking earlier.

I hadn't been this nervous since being with Neferterri last year, and she still made me nervous every time I was in her presence. But it was a different nervousness with shamise, probably because it was a different energy with the two of us.

I felt her teasing the insides of my thighs, and it was driving me insane because I wanted her to make me come. My clit was on the edge of explosion, and I couldn't stop screaming in my head for her to take me over the edge so I could come all over her face.

She must have read my body language and heard my silent pleas. shamise instinctively buried her face inside my lips and teased my clit until I couldn't take any more. I grabbed furiously at the comforter to keep from screaming loudly, but I was failing miserably as my tone became a series of oh-my-Gods and fuck-me-I'm-going-to-comes.

"i can feel you coming, baby; come for me," shamise directed, replacing her tongue with two fingers, voraciously finger-fucking my pussy into oblivion. "Give me that pussy, baby."

I was over the edge before I knew what was happening, and the wave that crashed over me left me feeling like I couldn't breathe. shamise spread my legs farther apart and moved up to my face and kissed me as I felt wave after wave consume my whole body. I shook uncontrollably as my body betrayed me in ways I couldn't control. I was in tears by the time my orgasm subsided.

"i'm glad you're staying with us." I was still trying to catch my breath as shamise pulled the comforter over us and snuggled with me. "But a few more nights like this and i might not want you to leave."

# FOURTEEN ⚭ RAMESSES

What a trip!

My mind was about taxed to its limits in dealing with Seti.

But it was worth the trip. Everything was going according to the plans that Amenhotep and I had set to motion. Plans to complete the circle and bring the balance back to the *Neb'net Maa'kheru* by having Seti and Osiris strike an accord and bury the animosity between them.

The "Society" had not been the same, nor had it been able to grow in number, since the two brothers had the tiff they'd had ten years ago. That was when keket, the slave who now served Osiris, had once been in service to Seti. Fate stepped in, as Seti was more into building his Poly family, while Osiris was more inclined to a more personal M/s relationship. keket was enamored with Osiris from first introduction and requested release from Seti a few months after that meeting. Although keket waited nearly six months before engaging Osiris for servitude, Seti never forgave his brother for the affront.

In my mind, things needed to change, and they were going to change.

The circle needed to be complete.

This was something I had wanted to do in payment to Amenhotep for helping me along my path, being the "father" to me in this realm. I felt I owed him that much, if not more.

I sat down in my first-class seat, put the headphones over my ears, and got ready to take the short flight back home.

There were a few things I needed to take care of there before I took a few days to relax a bit.

There was the pleasant and unexpected surprise of knowing shamise was back in town for good. At the same time, her path back into the House would not be a walk in the park.

Then there was the issue of Damian.

Something needed to come to fruition with him, and my Beloved knew it as much as I did. She had told me about the other day she'd spent with him, where he'd understood the nonsexual aspect of service he needed to handle, but there was something else that needed to be addressed, and it could only come from being in each other's space.

The tricky thing about having a male submissive in service to a male Dominant was there was always that barrier where the submissive got to the thought pattern that sex would eventually become a part of the dynamic. Frankly, there was not much truth to that, especially when both the Dominant and submissive were straight.

The past month, I had noticed a passive-aggressive attitude from him, like he was simply putting up with me in order to serve Neferterri. Nothing could enrage me more, particularly when we had removed female submissives for doing the exact same thing. But because he was new, I felt the need to give him the benefit of the doubt, perhaps even taking a more hands-on approach with him, letting him know this was not a bracketed dynamic.

He was due for a wake-up call, and I had no problems with providing it.

I had to be honest with myself before I figured out the path I needed Damian to take. Did I really want a male submissive in the

House? Could I deal with him the way Neferterri and I deal with the girls? Did I care what others thought about having him at my feet as sajira and shamise kneeled at my feet?

I had my own perceptions of myself I needed to worry about getting past and dispelling, so I could look at the man in the mirror and be okay with the man staring back at me.

As the plane began its ascent, I closed my eyes and sought out my thoughts from an outside perspective, trying to find the critic who might view me differently. I found him as the plane leveled off, accusing me of being "sweet" because I wanted a male to serve me.

The plane sped smoothly down the coastline as I verbally sparred with the critic about the ignorance he'd portrayed, putting me as a Dominant in some sort of "box" where I was supposed to be the omniscient and I should not be any more than what everyone expected me to be.

Who was he to tell me I was somehow "diminished" as a Dominant because I was willing to have a male in service to me? If anything, I was more than comfortable in my skin and my sexuality, and there was nothing he would be able to say to change my mind. It was my world, he had to adjust, and if he couldn't, fuck him.

Metaphorically speaking, of course…

I felt the plane bank left in its final approach into Georgia coming out of the Smoky Mountains, and by that time, my critic was blown from the discussion. All of the arguments being made were from an archaic perspective that didn't register for me in the twenty-first century.

The critic didn't agree with me. I was being foolish for trying to tarnish my reputation on a lesser male, in his opinion.

I sent a text in the midst of the debate to let Neferterri know Damian needed to pick me up from the airport.

He and I needed to have a little "chat," and it wouldn't be a pleasant one.

She texted back that he would be waiting at Baggage Claim.

Back and forth, the critic and I traded different points, trying to gain the upper hand, trying to keep the low blows to a minimum, knowing eventually it would get to that level anyway, so I braced myself for the epithets that would spew. I was quite surprised it didn't get there, though the discussion was heated nonetheless.

The flight attendant interrupted briefly to inform me the plane was reaching its final descent and I needed to put my seatbelt back on.

I obliged before heading back to the debate at hand.

Upon touching down, I bid the critic adieu and thanked him for the point of view, but I was secure in my dominance and I still controlled all I surveyed. He, in turn, thanked me and wished me well on the next opponent I would be facing in Damian; he did not envy the task I had ahead of me.

I nodded.

This would be an interesting ride home.

As we deplaned, I felt this rush of focus swirl around me, as though I clearly had the sight to do what needed to be done.

More importantly, how it would be done as well.

As I made my way to the escalators leading to baggage claim, I texted my Beloved one more time to let her know she would be a silent witness to a conversation that would be uncomfortable for her to hear.

Tonight, it was time to shit or get off the pot.

# FIFTEEN ⚭ SAJIRA

"Tell me what turns you on."

I was on the phone with my "Dom" again tonight, but for some reason, tonight was strangely different than the last few times I'd milked money from him.

The last time, he changed his demeanor on me, not being so abrasive, almost seductive. His voice was more commanding, and it caught me off-guard as my defenses were already up, thinking I knew where he was coming from.

My body began to respond to him the last time, and it freaked me out a little bit. I had told myself Daddy's voice would be the only one that could get me "there" over the phone, so I wasn't about to allow him to take me to the edge.

My "Dom" had other plans.

"You already know what turns me on, sir." I toyed with him, trying to keep him at bay as much as I could.

"Come on, sexy, I know everyone has a deep, dark fantasy they would like to have fulfilled." His voice got deeper as he talked, which slowly made me weak. "It's not like we'll ever be able to make it happen in person; wouldn't that be against the rules, Calypso?"

"Yes, sir, it would be against the rules." I tried to figure out why I was even considering whether it was against the rules in the first place. Against my better judgment, I confided in him. "I have fantasies about being raped."

"Mmmm, now we're getting somewhere," he said to me. "So, you fantasize about being taken against your will?"

"Yes, sir, I do." I was sinking deeper into the thoughts in my mind instead of hearing him. I didn't see the harm in telling him. I had no intentions of meeting him in person or anything like that, so I kept the fantasies in my head going. "The fear of it turns me on a lot, sir."

"Do you want to know who does this to you, or do you not want to know?" he asked, which piqued my curiosity further. He gave me the impression he'd done this before.

"Have you done it before? I mean, done a rape play scene before?" I wanted to know, but I wanted to deflect the question he'd asked more. Details he did not need to know about, and even though I'd already let the cat out of the bag, the less he knew from here on out, the better I felt.

"I had a partner of mine do it, said it was hot as hell when they did it," he answered. "She wanted to know it was him, but she didn't want to know when he decided to do it. He said it added to the adrenaline rush when he did take her."

I listened to him talk about the whole scene and it made me so wet, so embarrassingly wet, I wanted to end the call right then. But I couldn't resist listening to each detail, imagining I was the woman he was talking about.

"I can hear it in your voice, Calypso; it's turning you on," he said, picking up on the moaning I tried to keep to myself. "Are you playing in your pussy, Calypso?"

"Yes, sir, I am," I admitted. "May I continue to play in my pussy, please, sir? Telling me about the fantasy she fulfilled really has me wet."

"No, I don't think I will, Calypso," he abruptly answered. "I didn't tell you that you could play with your pussy."

I kept playing in my pussy, knowing it would upset him further. "I'm sorry, sir, but the way you sound when you tell the story, I can't help myself. Please, I want to hear more, please?"

I laid the begging on thick, and it seemed to have its effect on him, because he paused a moment before he uttered, "All right, Calypso, come for me, since you're already playing with your pussy."

I was already on the verge of an intense orgasm by the time he gave "permission" for me to climax over the phone for him.

I came so hard and screamed so loud I couldn't stop shaking. I heard him growling over the phone, letting me know my performance had gotten to him, too.

I kept the flow going, feeling another wave crashing over me immediately, causing me to scream even louder. *"Sir, my pussy's so wet for you; God, I can't stop coming!"*

All I heard from him was grunting and growling, which kept me going until my lips began to hurt from all the rubbing and spanking of my clit.

Once my orgasms subsided, I began to use the "pillow talk" time to see if he would let his guard down. I knew I was breaking the rules by the moment, but he had me open, and I wanted to see if he would indulge me some more. "What's your name, sir? You've never told me your name."

There was another pause on the phone, which made me wonder if I had gone too far with the question.

"My name is Deion." His response was cold and unfeeling. I immediately realized I'd gone too far. Before I could say another word, he snapped, "Are you happy now, bitch?"

*Click.*

# SIXTEEN ❀ NEFERTERRI

Getting the text from my Beloved was interesting.

But I couldn't say I didn't see it coming.

Damian had gotten too comfortable.

He was too comfortable around our girls…

He was too comfortable with the scene, and more importantly, he was getting too comfortable being under my control, but he wasn't doing what he needed to do to stay under my control.

He had done a good job a couple of days ago, I admitted, but he fell back into old patterns a little too quickly for my taste. His life as a submissive was not supposed to be comfortable, and I took some of the blame for that. His life as a submissive was to make my life comfortable, and to make the life of his Sir comfortable also.

Tonight was a make-or-break day, and he didn't even know it.

Not that I didn't see this coming, but there had to be a breaking point, and this was that point.

The text message I'd received said he would be calling me the minute Damian had collected him at baggage claim.

What Damian wouldn't know was how I would find out about the conversation they would soon have.

It was at times like this when most people usually say, *I wish I was a fly on the wall when this happened.*

Well, this time, I got to be a fly on the wall, with a cushy seat on my living room couch, sprawled out and half-naked because the kids wouldn't be home tonight. They were spending the night at their grandmother's house and wouldn't be back until morning.

I teased myself with the way the conversation would start. I didn't want to, but my curiosity got the best of me sometimes.

Would Damian act like nothing's going on and he's simply completing a task?

Would Ramesses start in on him right away?

Would he and Damian bullshit about sports before Ramesses blindsided him with questions?

Would Damian already know what the deal would be because he was the one picking Ramesses up instead of sajira, shamise, or one of the house slaves at NEBU?

The chime of my cell phone provided both the interruption to my thoughts and the answer to my questions all at the same time.

"Hi, baby, how was Your flight?" I sweetly spoke into the speaker phone of my cell.

"Hi, baby, the flight was short, thankfully, and Damian's with Me now." Ramesses instantly picked up on the tone of my voice. He spoke like the call was routine. "We're heading over to NEBU first before he drives Me home."

"Okay, baby, the girls should be home in the morning; they're at my mom's tonight," I told him, trying to give Damian the clue I was finishing the call. "Be careful on the way to NEBU, please?"

"We will, baby," he said before "hanging up" the phone.

The next series of sounds I heard were the two of them walking to the car; some words being spoken I couldn't make out, but that wasn't the part of the conversation I wanted to hear anyway. I went to the kitchen to get something to drink, and by the time I got back and settled into the couch to listen in, the conversation had begun.

"We need to figure out what your path will be within this House,

Damian. There are no two ways about it." I heard Ramesses cut to the chase.

"With all due respect, Sir, my path within the House is going along fine," Damian retorted. "Neferterri has been pleased with my growth thus far."

I was worried I would hear a sound similar to skin and bone connecting; he was seriously out of pocket talking to his Dominant in such a manner.

"See, young one, this is where you are failing to see the big picture." Ramesses was still calm, but I could hear the thunder rolling in the distance. "There are *two* Dominants in this House, and just because you've satisfied One, does not mean you've done your job. The girls know this all too well, or else they would not still be with us."

"i have tried to be of service to You, Sir. i dropped everything i was doing when Neferterri texted me to pick You up." Damian sounded agitated, and I hoped he would keep calm. With submissives, they can get really emotional when they feel their backs are against the wall. "What more do You want from me?"

"I understand that, and this particular occurrence is noticed, believe Me, but the previous month, you have been avoiding Me, and in order for you to function *properly* within this dynamic, *we have to get right with each other,*" Ramesses coldly stated. "So, when you get your ass off your shoulders and remember it's not about you, then we can continue this conversation."

There was a brief, yet painful, pause.

It certainly was going to get uglier from there. Damian tended to be a hothead. It's that passion that attracted me to him, but it could also be to his detriment. Ramesses didn't deal well with hot tempers. If anything, the calmer he got, the colder he became.

I imagined the car was probably thirty degrees colder than the abnormally warm eighty-nine degrees currently being reported in the city today.

"Ramesses, Sir, i apologize for forgetting my place," Damian quietly responded. "It was not my intention to snap at You, Sir."

I heard the quiet continue before anyone else spoke.

"Damian, I understand your frustration to a degree," I heard my husband begin. Whenever he started out like that, it's correction and pep-talk time. "I am not the Grim Reaper, contrary to the other submissive males' opinions."

That drew a chuckle out of Damian and a bit of a sigh of relief from me, because it felt like it was warming up in there. I hated the only thing I could do was listen and not say anything, but it was better than hearing about it after it was all over.

"Sir, if i may ask, what exactly would You have me do for You, to be in service to You?" Damian asked a very good question. "i mean, i know what Your Beloved wants out of me, but, let's face it, we're both straight, so, is there something different we should be doing?"

Ramesses kind of laughed a bit, and then he couldn't help but laugh a little bit more, like he had his own inside joke going on. I wondered what was going through his mind as I sat there continuing to listen in on this conversation.

"Damian, there is more to servitude than sex; I thought you would have figured that out by now," he bluntly stated. "What you do to serve Neferterri is one thing, and I'm sure you do more than serve Her sexually. There are duties that must be done for Me, such as your impromptu chauffeur duties you are handling right now. This is part of the reason why your training is so important."

"i understand, Sir." Damian nodded. "It actually makes me feel a whole lot better. Seeing how tiger serves when male Dominants are around, it was a little interesting, and it had me on edge when it came to how i translated how i was to serve You."

"you're still a rookie, so I figured something was amiss," Ramesses responded. "Now that we have figured out what the hell has been wrong with you the last month, we can move forward and get you into the fold."

"You mean, You actually are comfortable with having a male submissive serving You, Sir?" Damian asked again, letting the newness of his submission shine through again.

"I don't worry much about what the blogosphere says about different things, youngster." Ramesses's tone reminded me of the online infighting that went on when safi tried to file rape and kidnapping charges on Amenhotep. "If anything, most of those folks are too busy playing at what we do for real. It's the old saying, 'those that can, do…those that cannot, talk about it.'"

I laughed when I heard him say that because it did seem that way most of the time in watching the forums and blogs online. Some folks kept it positive and others kept a straight line, letting audiences know what we do was not for the faint of heart. But there were some who really make you scratch your head and wonder, *do you really believe what you're blogging about?*

"Understood, Sir, and i will do my best to follow along with that line of thinking because there's always the small doubt that creeps into your mind," Damian admitted. "We're almost to the office, Sir. Should i inform my Goddess of Your arrival there?"

"I don't think that will be necessary, Damian." I turned the mute off the speaker on my cell phone to answer. "So, do you accept your place at our feet, Damian?"

"Yes, my Goddess, i accept my place, and i am no longer afraid of that possibility anymore," Damian answered back. "Thank You both for being patient with me. i do hope to reward Your patience soon."

"I suspect you will quite soon, Damian," Ramesses spoke over the speaker as I heard them getting out of the car. "Of that I have no doubt."

# SEVENTEEN ⚬ SHAMISE

Oh, to be home again.

As much time and effort it took to get back to this point, I really thought I wouldn't be able to return. From what sajira explained to me, Daddy took my departure hard. I knew he cared deeply for me, and I loved him, too, but the last thing I wanted to do was hurt him or any one of my D/s family.

And yet, I knew Daddy would still have something in store for me, just to make me suffer a little for leaving. Especially when he knew I was aware that deep down, I really didn't want to leave.

But I felt it was something I needed to do at the time.

When I got married, almost from the moment that I said "I do," I'd made a mistake. I thought I wanted the family, the two kids, the husband with all the money to take care of things while I did nothing but take care of the house, take care of him when he got home from a hard day of work, and fuck him like a porn star the minute it was time to go to bed.

It's funny how reality slaps you in the face.

The first strike happened when he couldn't get it up the night of our wedding. We did a quickie thing in Vegas, followed by a "romantic" consummation of the marriage in one of the spacious suites inside of the MGM Grand.

I know how I'm used to getting fucked, and my new husband

wasn't measuring up at all by comparison. The way Daddy handled me, or his friends handled me...well, I thought I made sure he could keep up. I blamed it on nerves for him, because he was handling business before we got married. The moment we got to L.A., it was like night and day, so I wondered why he wouldn't handle things now.

The second strike happened about a month later. I was already having an itch to come back home to Atlanta. He was slowly cutting off anyone willing to befriend me, male or female, and insisted that, unless he was taking me out, which happened about three times a week, I didn't need to get out, learn the city, or anything that would allow me to embrace L.A. I was fine because he was *finally* taking care of business in bed, and the bills were still getting paid, so, there was nothing that really had me going a bit.

That was before Stephanie showed up.

That should have been strike three, but there was a bit of a twist in that story.

Stephanie was not who you think "she" was. She was actually a she-male, post-op, and hung like Justin Slayer. Don't tell Daddy, but I loved, loved, *loved* Justin Slayer.

I won't get off on a tangent just yet, so let me focus.

Stephanie came to the house about two months after we got married. Out of the blue, she knocked on the door and gave me the once-over after I opened the door to find out who this strange, but strikingly beautiful "girl," was at my door.

Until she told me she was looking for my husband because she had been fucking him since before I married.

Again, that should have been strike three.

But it wasn't.

☥

The next month after that was interesting.

Stephanie would spend time with me while my husband was at work; meanwhile, my husband would come up with convenient excuses as to why he needed to work late. I knew Stephanie was with him at night, and the location would always be different; she would confide in me on the mornings after they were together.

By that point, I was already filing for divorce in California. Community property state…

And he had millions available to take, with the minor complication of a prenuptial agreement that had an infidelity clause written in, paying me millions if he were to cheat on me.

Hey, I didn't say he was smart, just a good fuck.

The final straw actually didn't come from me, but from Stephanie. She was tired of sharing him, but she couldn't let me go.

I was tired of both of them and wanted to go home to my family. Millions of dollars richer, yes, but I was tired of them both.

Stephanie confronted him a couple of weeks before I filed, telling him he had better get rid of me or else she was going to tell me about their affair. Sure, it was going to cost him, but it would have been better than to suffer the embarrassment at work that he was with a "freak."

That night, he told me everything.

My Goddess would have been proud of the award-winning performance that I gave, complete with the crocodile tears.

The next morning, I was signing transaction papers into a bank account that placed five million dollars into my newly opened checking account, and twenty million into the newly opened savings account.

I told you he wasn't too bright.

But I guess I wasn't too bright, either. I wasted precious time I could never get back.

Stephanie tried to talk me into staying in L.A. so we could continue seeing each other behind his back, but I was turned off by the clingy nature she had begun to display, and that was something I couldn't deal with.

So, here I was, relaxing in the guest bedroom of Ice and sajira's home, basking in the glow of a very, very passion-filled night.

But I was restless.

I needed my Master and Mistress to put me to sleep *properly*.

I knew that wasn't going to happen, though. Considering it was nearly two in the morning, and even though the kids were probably spending the weekend at their grandmother's house, I knew better than to wake up the house, so, I logged in on my laptop to try and find some stuff to put me to sleep.

I logged in to yahoo messenger to catch up with some of the people I was able to connect with while I was in L.A. I knew most of them were still awake, since it was only after eleven out there.

I was in a friendly chat with a submissive friend in San Diego when...

**lord_ramesses:** *good morning, little one. Shouldn't you be in bed?*

I froze.

He was right.

It was well past my curfew.

**scarlett.flame:** *yes, Daddy, i am in bed. i was a little restless.*

**lord_ramesses:** *that doesn't give you cause to break your curfew, Scarlett*

**scarlett.flame:** *i'm sorry, Daddy, i did not want to break curfew, but i'm really, really wet right now*

**lord_ramesses:** *then ask permission to release that tension, Scarlett. you know the House rules*

He had me there, and we both knew it.

My hands instinctively moved between my legs, feeling the heat that hadn't waned since sajira left me to go to bed. I heard his voice in my ear, and I couldn't resist the nasty thoughts his voice commanded of me.

Daddy must have felt me calling out for him because my cell phone rang a few seconds later.

"Mmmmm, hi, Daddy, how are You tonight?" I purred into the phone.

"I see you two had a pretty good night tonight." I heard the bass in his voice, and the rush I felt flow through me was indescribably overwhelming. "So, it must have been important for you to break your curfew."

I swallowed hard as I felt my fingers getting slicker by the second, just from hearing his voice. "Yes, Daddy, my body is on fire after playing with sajira a little while ago. i really need to release again, if i am allowed to do so, Daddy."

The pause over the phone caused my heart to race. I normally didn't give in to my libido unless it was commanded, but I had to admit to myself that not being held to House protocol had made me lazy. I was used to indulging in my urges when I felt like it, and I knew that's not what my Dominants required of me, nor was it House protocol. I immediately felt guilty I was disappointing him by even admitting I wanted to give in without express permission.

"No, Scarlett, I don't think so, but I do have an idea of how you can please Me," I heard him speak finally after what felt like an eternity of silence. "Do you know that your soon-to-be sister is doing a side gig as a phone sex operator?"

That question hit me, and not in a bad way. "Yes, Daddy, she mentioned that while we were catching up earlier today."

"Good, because I have a task for you, and I have a feeling it will be something good for you." As much as I could anticipate his next command, I didn't dare speak it for fear that I would be incorrect. I had been gone almost six months, and while the connection was strengthening again with both of them, it hadn't yet gotten back to where it once was.

"What do You command of me, m'Lord?" I went into high protocol, as I heard the tone in his voice become more rigid, more demanding. It made me wetter by the moment, and I tried to keep my wits about me, in case he mentioned something to intentionally throw me off.

"you will join your sister in working the side gig," he began. "It's not like you need the money, so consider it a phase of your training and another condition of your re-entry into the House."

I didn't know whether to jump for joy at that moment or try to make it sound like I was "okay" with it all, like it was no big deal. My Daddy and my Goddess know about my desire to be exhibitionist in any and all ways possible. In fact, it's one of the reasons why I kneeled before them to be a part of the House in the first place: to be shown off, anywhere, anytime.

I tried hard to compose myself, but the excitement in my voice couldn't completely be contained. "Yes, m'Lord, i understand Your command of me, and i will do as You command."

"Good girl, I knew you would."

*God, why does it make me melt to hear him say those two words?*

"I will leave it to sajira to make the necessary steps to get you in the loop. Now, I have one more task for you to complete before bed, little one."

"Yes, m'Lord?" I queried.

"I want you to come for Me," he flatly commanded, and my hand instinctively moved to my clit. "I want you to tell Me about it, in detail, tomorrow when your Goddess and I call you in the morning to discuss your full-time job at NEBU."

"Yes, m'Lord, thank You for allowing me to release," I replied. My voice dripped with sex as I desperately tried to send that sexual energy in his direction in the hope he would stay on the phone a little while longer to hear an explosion tailor-made for him, and only him.

"Good night, My Scarlett." His voice deepened, which only spurred my oncoming orgasm. "Make it a good one."

I hung up the phone, my fingers already completely coated with my juices, thanks to him. It only took a few more minutes before I screamed out his name with my legs clamped tightly over fingers furiously pushing wave after wave of an orgasm most people only wished they could have.

An orgasm so intense it immediately put me to sleep.

God, it's good to be home again.

# EIGHTEEN ✿ RAMESSES

"Everything is going according to plan."

My Beloved expressed her reservations with going through with this phase of the plan, but the way I saw it, it was needed to move things to the next level. When we first had decided to travel down this path, I had made it clear this was not something that was needed, but it was critical to growth. There has to be pain in order for growth to happen. In the immortal words of Frederick Douglass, "If there is no struggle, there is no progress."

For the past few weeks, whispers began popping in my ear and innuendo started showing up on the message boards online, making me pause, but making me more determined to take action. There was no choice in the matter. Things have happened that have set the wheels in motion, and it was my responsibility to see things to their fruition.

Lessons needed to be learned.

"Very good, so we need to step up the pressure a little more, to let them know we mean business."

"Don't worry, they won't see it coming." The voice on the phone went silent for a moment before asking the next question. "Was it a good idea to involve her? If this backfires, it could be a world of pain inflicted for no reason."

"Heavy is the head that wears the crown, remember?" I laughed to combat the uneasiness I felt. My Beloved felt there was a better way to deal with this, but I was determined to make a statement and nip this in the bud once and for all. "Your responsibility is to execute, unless You feel You can't handle it?"

"You forgot who I am, partner. I'm not a rookie." I felt the tension in his tone, but I wasn't about to relent. Besides, I was used to someone trying to be the "devil's advocate" and try to talk me out of some supposed bad idea that they didn't have the foresight to see the conclusion before it happened. That was the difference between the other folks and me: I had strength of conviction in my abilities as a Dominant.

"For the record, in this matter, You are a rookie, so You need to follow My lead. Don't worry, once this all goes down, I'm going to enjoy the look on Your face when You see how a boss does things."

"Yeah, yeah, Boss, I'm simply echoing Your wife's concerns. This could be bad; it might not end well."

"Then I'll take the chance. Like I said before, when You're on top, You have to make the hard call. This, everything we've been doing, was never meant to be a peaches-and-cream type of ride. If You don't have the stomach for it, You're welcome to bow out; I won't take offense."

"All right, on to the next phase, but don't be surprised if it spooks them."

"I won't be surprised. In fact, I know exactly how this is going to go down. Oh, and when the big reveal happens, I want You to be there."

"I wouldn't miss it for the world."

# NINETEEN ⚭ NEFERTERRI

"Neferterri, how wonderful of You and Your boi to join us."

I heard Sinsual calling from the great room as we stepped inside of her home. tiger led us into the area where the rest of the group had congregated. Damian was with me, a little nervous as this was his first time being in an atmosphere like this. I wanted it to be the two of us this time, since sajira usually attended these meetings with me.

We walked down the hallway, making a brief stop in the kitchen to grab a snack and some drinks before settling down in the great room. Once there, tiger moved back to his spot and position at Sinsual's feet. I took my seat in my usual spot near Sinsual in a recliner, commanding Damian to his spot to kneel at my right side.

I didn't speculate about where Ice was, even though his Mistress usually required both of her bois to be in attendance. He was out of town on business, according to sajira, so there was no need to ask her about his whereabouts.

We usually get together as Dominas about once a month on Saturday afternoons to discuss matters specific to what we have to deal with within the Fetish and BDSM community as women, regardless of color. What made the get-together so unique was that Sinsual actually had a video conference set up through her flat-panel television and PC, linking with her webcam with other Dominas throughout various areas of the country. They're quite entertaining, depending on the topic we choose.

This month's topic was how our submissives and slaves deal within our respective dynamics. Considering Kemet-Ka was a rare Poly dynamic, I was sure to become the epicenter of the discussion.

Sinsual was here, as was Blaze as always. Mistress Ethereal was a new face to the group, relocating here from Texas, and a couple of other ladies who normally joined us sporadically from time to time. Lady Hatshepsut joined us from Vegas through the video conference room, along with Dominas from L.A., Tampa, New York, D.C. and a few other places. In total today, about fifteen or so of us were in attendance. I guessed the topic had people very interested in coming in.

"Ladies, I want to thank You all for coming," Sinsual started, grabbing her wireless keyboard to type the topic into the conference room so everyone would be on the same page. "I'm sure the majority of You know of each other, so, we can keep the pleasantries at a minimum."

The conversation moved as it always did, at a pretty good pace, not too fast, not too slow to the point to where it came to a standstill. There were flare-ups every now and again, which will happen when different dynamics come into play, along with differing perspectives and ideologies. But all in all, the discussion kept a pace that inspired some new ideas and reinforced some old ways.

One question was placed for me to answer by a Domina in New York, Lady Norene. Ramesses and I encountered her last year at one of the conferences in the New Jersey area. It was on topic, but completely off topic, and I wasn't sure if she was naturally curious or if she was really perturbed.

It didn't help she was staring a little too intensely at Damian through the webcam feed, and it wasn't a look I took too kindly to.

"Neferterri, I am curious to know, how do You maintain Your Dominance within Your House, especially considering You are married to a Dominant male?"

Her eyes narrowed as she continued to stare at Damian, and I could feel him moving closer to me, as though he needed protection from her stare. I rubbed his temple and let him know I was still there and something needed to be done about this woman now.

"I'm not quite sure I understand what You are asking Me, Lady Norene." I tried to redirect the focus. "What does My marriage to Ramesses have to do with the current discussion? Our submissives are able to deal within the House quite well at present."

"Quite honestly, I think it flows with this discussion, Lady Neferterri," Norene continued. "Considering You have a new boi at Your feet now, I assume Ramesses had to sign off on his entry into the House. So, I wonder, how does Your new boi serve Him? I don't remember Ramesses having any homosexual or bisexual tendencies."

Something in my mind clicked, and as much as I wanted to maintain my sense of decorum, this bitch stepped over the line. The sexuality of the men in my life were none of her concern, and for her to throw it out there like it was okay to banter about with it, infuriated me.

Okay, so she wanted to take the gloves off? That's fine. I was actually used to the women up North having certain attitudes about the "way" of things.

But my men were not to be fucked with.

"I'm assuming You know how My dynamic works, Norene?" I kept the tone civil, but I was ready to shred through her. "Because if You do, then You know the men in this House are heterosexual.

How Damian serves his Sir does not generate sexual overtones. May I ask why You felt the need to take the discussion down this path?"

"Well, I won't lie to You; I am curious, Neferterri." Norene tried not to let on from her webcam that she had some disdain toward me. It wasn't hard to figure that one out, though. Her body language gave her away. "I mean, who has the final say in the decisions and the vision of the House? There has to be a hierarchy, right? Everyone that know You both knows that Ramesses tends to be the Alpha and Omega within the community down there in Atlanta. Now that Amenhotep has relocated and stepped away from the scene, Ramesses is the man now."

Now the bitch wasn't playing fair. Also, it was obvious from her intent on focusing on my property, she was going to continue to be blatantly disrespectful, so I dropped my leg over Damian's shoulder in a show of territorial force. I saw Norene's eyes widen for a minute, but she didn't change her posture.

If she wanted to play dirty, I had plenty where that first statement had come from.

She sat back in her chair like she thought it was over.

I was just getting started.

"I don't think so, and I don't know where You're getting Your information from." I retorted, showing my anger at that moment. There were always some people who felt the need to think because Ramesses was constantly in the limelight and in the public eye that somehow, he was the one who handled everything within the House.

Nothing could be further from the truth.

"I have some news for You, dear." I switched my body position to face her flush, so there was no mistaking my conviction. "The House of Kemet-Ka is handled by two Dominants; One does not outrank or outflank the other, and I handle things in the House as the final verdict, just as He does. When our submissives…emphasis on *OUR*...serve the two of us, together or as individuals, make no mistake they do not always come to Him to get the final say on matters or commands. Does that clear up any other issues You have in Your mind regarding how the House of Kemet-Ka is run?"

Suddenly, pins could be heard hitting the carpet.

Sinsual stepped in after a few seconds to break the ice building in the room.

"Norene, we are grown women here; if You have an issue with Neferterri personally, I think You are woman enough to express it in a more discretionary manner. Do You have an issue with the Poly dynamic Neferterri has dominion over?"

"Actually, I take issue with the fact that She is here in a de-facto capacity, for lack of a better term," Norene answered. "She's not the head of Her dynamic, and it fucks with My perspective of Female Supremacy. I tolerate Ramesses in all honesty because He is an honorable Dominant and He has a respect for Dominas and Mistresses and Female Masters alike, but when we have discussions like this where Her opinion can skew the prevailing thought, someone had to say something."

"So, You believe I'm a lesser Dominant because I share power with My husband?" I was ready to spit fire now. "How dare You presume some sort of diminished respect for Me because I don't fit Your Supremacist ideals? And for the record, respect begets respect, bitch. You have to give to get, and right now, You will do right by Me to keep Your thoughts and opinions about something You know *nothing* about to Yourself from now on, since You cannot respect a different flow of a power exchange. Are we clear?"

I locked eyes with her through the satellite feed, and I saw something in that exchange that hadn't shown up before.

She was hurting. As much as she tried to hide it, I could see it in her expression.

Call me a Sadist if you want, but at that point, I was out for blood, and there weren't too many people on this planet who could cause me to call off the dogs.

And even those two would have hell trying to at this particular moment.

I continued the stare-down, negating the fact that she'd surrendered the fight to me. Her eyes softened, taking one last look at Damian before she completely changed her demeanor.

My body twitched, and I wanted to say something further, to finish her off, but I felt a calming hand across my forearm.

"Okay, ladies, enough." Sinsual tried to diffuse the discussion. "Norene, we all know what Your thoughts are and Your position, but to disrespect a fellow Domina is unacceptable, and to attack a Dominant who cannot be here to defend Himself is even more egregious. Your questions and accusations are baseless, as You have admittedly spent very little time around their dynamic to espouse any disdain toward Neferterri. If You wish to continue to participate in these conferences, a swift apology is in order."

There was more silence as all eyes turned in Norene's direction.

I felt Damian move between my legs, and it was at that moment, I'd nearly forgotten he was at my feet. He placed a kiss on my inner thigh and then positioned himself to massage my now bare feet. The sensation took some of the steam from my anger as I silently nodded for him to continue.

Finally, Norene changed her tone and spoke to me. "My dear Neferterri, please accept My apology for the way I attacked You. I know it may sound hollow after what I said, but I have a great respect for what You and Ramesses have put together. It is a rare thing indeed, and I should not have tried to belittle it so fervently."

Still feeling the pleasure Damian brought through his foot massage, I reluctantly left his gaze to accept Norene's apology. "Norene, I accept Your retraction, and there are no hard feelings...actually, that's a lie; there are some hard feelings, and I'm still heated. I can't imagine what possessed You, but hopefully, if You have issues You would like to speak to Me about in the future, I will hope You will bring them to Me privately rather than subject others to something that was not warranted."

Sinsual spoke to end the conference. "Ladies, it has been a pleasure, although it was rather spirited toward the end, and I do hope to see You here in a couple of weeks for the grand reopening of NEBU, formally known as the Palace."

☥

"What the hell was that about?"

There were a lot of us in the great room of Sinsual's home who were at a loss for words as we continued some casual conversation after the conference was over.

"She's never been that blatantly disrespectful before today," Blaze mentioned. "I do wonder what got into Her."

"Or what hasn't," one of the Dominas in live attendance, Goddess Hera, made mention. "She's been in a Dominant frenzy over the past few weeks. One of My friends up there says She has been frustrated at the male and female submissives who have spurned Her advances for acquisition or play."

Damian had finally finished my foot massage when he silently tapped my wrist, which was the simple protocol we'd set up for him when he wanted to speak.

"Yes, Damian, would you like to speak?" I stated for the room to hear.

"Yes, Goddess, i think i know the reason for Her outburst."

"With My permission, you may speak," I allowed.

"Well, Lady Norene began speaking to me around the same time that You and i began speaking, Goddess," Damian explained. "She was quite aggressive, if i am allowed to say so."

"Yes, you are fine, Damian; go on," I encouraged. This information brought some things to light, and I was interested in finding out what had transpired between them.

"Yes, Goddess," he replied. "Per Your protocol, i informed m'Lady i was also speaking to You on a casual level at that time, and She felt i was being un-sub-like because i didn't focus my attention on Her and Her alone."

The more I listened to what Damian said, the more I acknowledged one simple fact: regardless of gender, Dominants tended to be extremely territorial, even during the consideration period. I took a different tact when it came to submissives who were being considered. I likened it to "dating" and figuring out if the fit was best within the House. At the end of the day, especially in a Poly D/s household, the amalgamation of personalities was of paramount priority. Not everyone thought the way Ramesses and I did, especially the monogamous sect in the BDSM community. Once a submissive was being placed under consideration, it was almost like they were off-limits until the consideration period was over.

"She became more verbally abusive, saying i didn't deserve to be in a House that didn't care about me because You were Poly with multiple submissives," he recounted, which only upset me more that he went through this. "i tried to respectfully disagree with Her, but She felt i would be better off with Her because it was a monogamous dynamic and the focus would be on me. i admitted i might have my moments where i might crave attention, but She took the admission as me being a brat and trying to get my way. After a while, i had no other choice but to block Her,

Goddess. i know it sounds terrible, but She made me uncomfortable around Her, and i didn't feel compelled to speak with Her any longer."

"So, I guess seeing you at My feet might have been the final straw," I concluded. "I knew you were speaking with another Dominant, Damian, but I guess I should have asked who that Dominant was, in case we encountered Her in the future, after you'd made your decision to kneel to Me and become a part of this House."

"Lesson learned, My dear," Sinsual explained. "There was no way to know Norene would be that unstable just by seeing you two together, so no need to beat yourselves up over it. She'll have to get over it in Her own way. Now, let's enjoy the rest of this lovely late-spring weather and take this outside."

We all walked out to the deck in the backyard to relax in the sun. We let the submissives congregate while the three of us got a chance to talk amongst ourselves.

"Your boi handled You pretty well after You took target practice." Blaze chuckled, referring to my exchange with Norene. "I saw his hands on Your feet while Sin was berating Norene. he seems to be picking up on the silent protocol pretty well."

"Yes, ever since he and Ramesses had their discussion, it's like night and day." I tried to contain the smirk on my face, but I was failing miserably. I couldn't contain the excitement in my voice. "It's like he's been reading a lot, absorbing and putting it into practice as quickly as he can."

"I'm still sore at You for not telling Me about the potential he had." Sin cut her eyes at me in mock anger. "I would have gladly let You have Ice so I could groom that fine specimen You have now. I swear, that boi is beginning to work My last nerve with some of the antics he puts Me through."

"Quit complaining, Sin. You wanted Ice and pursued him hard, and You got what You wanted, which was why You gave Damian up so easily in the first place," Blaze interjected. She laughed at the feigned outrage Sin tried to put on. "I should be the one acting a fool because You decided to drop him in Her lap, but I'm not one to hold a grudge, Sis."

I laughed it off, not really caring one way or the other how Damian was placed in my path. I was going to milk it for all it was worth—good, bad, or indifferent. They could be irritated with each other all they wanted. It had nothing to do with me because I didn't have them coming at me left and right like I was the second coming of whatever Amazon Goddess was hot right now. I only hoped they would stop talking about it long enough to enjoy the scenery with all these beautiful bois in Sin's backyard.

tiger approached us, getting a silent nod from Sinsual to ask me a question. "m'Lady, might i ask Your permission to speak privately with Your Damian?"

My eyebrow rose slightly, trying to gauge where tiger's inquiry was coming from.

"Yes, you have My permission, tiger," I replied, curious as to what was on his mind. "May I ask what you're sensing that has you asking to speak privately?"

"m'Lady, if it pleases You, i noticed some tendencies i would like to explore a little bit," tiger mentioned, sounding confident that he might be right. "Some of the other bois can feel it, too, but You know how we can be when there are no Dominants looking around."

Yeah, I knew all too well, and I couldn't contain my curiosity to see how far this might go. "By all means, tiger, but do so with caution. you might be right, but then again, you might be wrong. I don't want your Mistress pissed at Me because My boi gave you a black eye."

tiger gave a knowing wink. "Believe me, m'Lady, if i'm right, a black eye will be the last thing he gives me."

☥

I noticed Damian was especially agitated on the drive home, and not necessarily in a bad way. He looked like he wasn't sure if he should have been ashamed of what had happened between him and tiger or turned on.

We watched with vested interest after Damian and tiger came from the private conversation they'd had, and Sin noted the flushed look on Damian's face, which let her know tiger had tried him.

The sated look on tiger's face let us know he was right in his instincts.

He kept playfully touching Damian as the other submissives were talking amongst themselves and out of our earshot. Damian's body language definitely piqued my interest on a few levels. He never once shied away.

Interesting, very interesting...

I could use this for a surprise I had in store for him for the grand reopening night. The thought produced delicious shivers down my spine.

My sadistic side took over again, and I wanted to see how much more uncomfortable I could make him as he drove me home.

"So, Damian, how did you enjoy your first real-time atmosphere in a nonsexual setting?" I asked, sliding my fingers onto his knee.

I saw him tighten his grip on the steering wheel, and the deep sigh let me know he was ripe for the taking. "Goddess, i enjoyed myself a lot, even though Lady Norene almost ruined it, if i am allowed to say so."

I moved my hands inside of his thigh, feeling the bulge through the khakis he'd worn. I kept moving under the fabric, feeling the bulge underneath now, a slick smile on my face as I kept teasing him to give me details I wanted between him and tiger.

"So, what did he do to you?"

"he asked me to feel his dick, Goddess."

"Did you enjoy how it felt in your hands?"

"i'm embarrassed to say, Ma'am." He tried to concentrate on the road, but it proved more difficult by the minute. You would have thought he was holding on to the steering wheel as if his very life depended on it.

"your embarrassment is not My concern, Damian," I roughly answered, still teasing him under his shorts. His dick was rock solid now, and I tried to contain the smile that was slowly expressing itself across my face. "I want an answer to My question, and I will not ask again."

"Yes, Goddess, i liked how it felt in my hands." Damian held back tears as he said it. "i wanted to do more, if i am allowed to say, Ma'am."

"Good boi," I told him, trying to give him a slight bit of encouragement, providing him with a safe environment to express himself. He had some trepidation about what had happened to him, and I didn't want to make him feel ashamed. If anything, he played right into my hands.

"What does this mean, Goddess? i have never felt those type of urges before." He was panicking, and it was expected. After all, he didn't think he had it in him. "i feel like i don't know what to think anymore and my body is betraying me."

"you're missing the point, Damian." I gave his length a gentle squeeze to return his focus. "I, your Goddess, am not having a

problem with what you have experienced. Knowing this information, you should have no problem with what you have experienced."

"i know, Ma'am, but…"

I cut my eyes at him, shutting him down quickly. "But, nothing,
Damian," I scolded, my hands still firmly around his shaft. "What
you are experiencing is normal, because your mind is trying to
process it, but it will pass in time; I promise you. your body responded
to the stimulus, and the fact that you still want more says a lot."

"Yes, Goddess." He finally released his death grip on the steering
wheel as we approached the house. "my body is Yours to command,
in any way that You command. i will do as You command."

He was in need of a release—his body felt tense to me—but I
was not in the mood to provide that release, so I texted one of my
girls at *Liquid* to see if she was at home.

I had a favor to cash in.

When I received the text back from her, stating she was at home
and understood what I wanted her to do, I turned my attention to
Damian. "I want you to go to this address, Damian. When you
get there, there will be a woman that answers the door. The only
thing that you need to say to her is 'my Goddess sent me to take
care of you.' Do you understand Me?"

"Yes, my Goddess, i understand, and i will do as You command."
He tried to mask his lust at hearing the commands from my lips,
but I heard everything I needed to hear.

I got out of the car after receiving a kiss on my hand from him,
waiting to see the sad, puppy dog eyes. After he drove away, I
flipped out my cell phone to call Sin to let her know she was right.
He was mine.

He was ready to make the transition.

# TWENTY ⊗ SHAMISE

I was nervous as we rode.

I didn't know exactly where we were going and that was mostly what made me nervous. Oh yes, I completely trusted my Daddy, really I did. But he was so cryptic about this trip. He just told me he and Neferterri loved me and it was time to make good on the "one condition" he alluded to while he was out of town. I desperately wanted to quiz him about what those plans were, but I bit my tongue rather than question him.

He watched me squirming in my seat as he drove and smiled to himself. He knew I was dying to ask where we were going and what the condition upon my complete surrender was, but he would be proud of me for not asking. I hadn't forgotten my teachings. I was becoming more obedient and submissive and more at home with each passing day.

I was getting frustrated because I couldn't figure out exactly where we were in downtown Atlanta. I admit I didn't know the city very well, even though I'd lived there since high school. This was obviously a trendy part of town. I think it might have been Little Five Points. There were coffee shops and chic little boutiques. The area was entirely made up of small businesses catering to a young, hip, urban crowd.

Still, Daddy pulled in and parked at a small lot at the end of a long row of shops. I strained my neck trying to see the signs of all the shops in the row. He parked the car and came around to open my door. I had forgotten how much of a gentleman he was.

He led me down the row of shops and smiled as he caught me ogling the fashions in the windows. He stopped in front of the final destination and gripped my hand a little tighter. He waited for my reaction as I read the lettering on the window:

*XXotic Body Art: Original Tattoos and Exotic Piercings*

The rules of the game changed, and I knew it. I looked at him with genuine fear in my eyes.

"Relax, little one. There's no point in resisting now. After all, you did say that I could name My condition." He smirked at me as he tugged on my hand, pulling me inside with him.

The words *oh shit* popped in my head as I cleared my throat and swallowed hard and managed to smile weakly at him. More than anything else, I only wanted to please my owners, but I was desperately curious about what he had in mind about the condition I so naively agreed to.

Daddy led me into the shop. I was relieved to see it was well-kept and attractive, but then again, I never had to worry about that with him. Daddy was particular about where he conducted business. There was a glass case of jewelry under a counter and framed artwork on the walls. Behind the glass counter, a long hallway led straight back past several doors on either side.

There were no other customers in the store. A broad-shouldered man who looked as thick as a brick wall was behind the counter. Another man was mounting new artwork onto the walls. A third man was moving some boxes in the hallway.

Daddy went up to the counter confidently and gave his name to the man, adding, "I have an appointment."

The man smiled and shook his hand. He introduced himself as David. "Oh yes, we were expecting you."

David looked me over from top to bottom, and while I had no issue with him admiring my body, his smile had me on edge a little, like he thought I was the next entrée on the menu at the buffet. I didn't feel uncomfortable about it, though. The one thing Ramesses and Neferterri instilled in their girls was a sense of confidence in the way that they presented themselves.

I wore a very short skirt with no panties, a halter top, and sandal heels, as I was commanded. I knew my nipples stood out prominently for all the men to see clearly through the fabric. But I didn't meet any of the men's stares. My place was to be demure and submissive.

"Let's get started," David said as he gestured the way down the hallway.

We followed David to the room, and with the way the men continued to ogle me as I walked past them, I had no doubt this was part of Daddy's design. If he wanted to, he could have had the store deserted, but this was his way of reasserting his dominion over me. No matter who was around, my focus should always be on him.

"Right into room three, please." He called to one of his coworkers and told him he was going to the back to do a "procedure." I clung tightly to Daddy's hand as he led me down the hall. He was very clandestine about the entire encounter as David opened the door to room three. Daddy led me inside.

The room was clean and sterile, like a doctor's examination room. I found it interesting to see an exam table. To me, it looked like the exam room at my gynecologist's office, except the table was tilted and curved, more like a chair. There were two rolling arm-less desk chairs, a rolling stool, a counter, a sink, and some cabinets.

David entered behind us and talked about me instead of to me, arousing my wondering if he was "in the know" or not. "Okay, get her undressed and in the exam chair, so I can see what we are working with."

Startled, I looked at Daddy, but he only smiled and winked at me, which somehow put me at ease. With sure hands only he had, Daddy pulled my shirt over my head and pulled my skirt down, whisking it all away along with my sandals. I stood naked in the middle of the room.

Now, a few years ago, I would have been embarrassed to be naked in public with this strange man looking at me. But as I lowered my eyes, I could see Daddy's erection. That calmed me down because I knew I was pleasing him immensely. I stood up a little taller and straighter and smiled at him.

Daddy glanced over at David. The man's tongue was nearly hanging out as he looked at me. David had this grin on his face like he'd hit the jackpot, staring at this caramel-skinned woman in front of him, but Daddy never lost his cool about it. This wasn't the first time we'd been out as a family and other men were busy gawking at his prized possessions. But I knew how Daddy was, too, and if he felt the need to shut a situation down, he would do exactly that.

David broke into my thoughts. "Okay, get her up into the chair."

I smiled as he led me to the exam chair. I scooted my ass up onto the end and leaned back. I picked up one leg at a time and placed my feet into the stirrups. My face was red at having my pussy exposed, but I was wet as hell knowing that anything could happen at any moment.

For all I knew, Daddy would let David fuck me, as payment for the piercing.

Not that I minded all that much. For a white man, David was ruggedly handsome, and he reminded me of one of those ex-Marines that still kept in amazing shape well long after serving. Now that I thought about it, he reminded me of Jason Statham. Imagining him in his dress blues got me even wetter as David sat on the rolling stool between my legs and pushed the stirrups farther apart until my pussy was spread lewdly in front of him.

He didn't touch me, but leaned in close to examine my folds. Now my face burned with embarrassment—not because David was inspecting me, but because I was highly aroused and Daddy didn't give me permission. I secretly hoped he couldn't smell the deliciously musky scent I gave off, but part of me wanted him to get a whiff of what he couldn't have…unless Daddy commanded me to.

For a moment, I felt David's warm breath on my pussy as he leaned in close. My heart raced. Was Daddy actually going to let this stranger have his way with me???

"Okay, Kane, I have the notes from our phone conversation. I wrote down exactly what you want done. Physically, I see no problems. All we have to do is negotiate a price."

Daddy raised his eyebrows, but I couldn't tell if he was going along with the dialogue or not. After all, David called him by his first name. "But you already quoted me a price on the phone."

David smiled. "Well, yes, but that price is negotiable."

"Oh, how so?" Daddy queried.

"Well," David suggested while looking at me, "this is a nice piece of ass. Let me keep her overnight and play with her. You can pick her up tomorrow and the procedure will be absolutely free."

I almost couldn't stifle the laugh, but I didn't find it so funny anymore after I saw that Daddy looked as if he were considering the offer.

My heart pounded through my chest, wishing he would make the decision and get it over with so I could prepare myself. Despite the hesitation, I knew my Daddy too well. He could be sadistic, devilishly sadistic. He probably felt my anxiety and enjoyed every minute of it, making me suffer needlessly because his mind was made up several minutes ago.

I hated that I loved him for that, and I loved that he didn't care whether I hated it or not.

In the end, it was not about me.

After another moment's hesitation, he placed his hand in the air, signaling his refusal of the offer. "As tempting as the offer is, that's not happening, David."

David counteroffered, "Okay, just let me fuck her now and the procedure will be free. All you have to pay for is the materials."

Once again, he hesitated. "No, sorry, David, she is my property."

David shook his head. "Okay, okay, but how about a fifty percent discount on labor if she sucks my dick?"

Daddy still shook his head. "No, sorry, and quite frankly, I'm done with this negotiation, like there was ever one to begin with."

I will admit I was slightly disappointed I wouldn't be able to "perform." After being under wraps with my now ex-husband and not being my true exhibitionist self, I was looking to jump back in with both feet and immerse myself within my wantonness again.

David sighed and seemed to give up. "Okay, let me tell you what has to be done and we can get started. You realize she has to be fully aroused for this procedure. I need her clit swollen to its fullest. However, you can't let her reach orgasm because the swelling will subside too soon. So, you have to arouse her and keep her on the edge of orgasm while I do the piercing."

The words roared into my ears.

Daddy was having my clit pierced.

Okay, I was officially worried I had gotten myself in deeper than I was willing to go. I bit my lip and felt hot tears flood from my eyes down my cheeks. I knew Daddy wanted to make me completely his and Neferterri's property. But I was afraid of the pain, and I didn't know how to deal with that fear.

Daddy leaned over and kissed away my tears as David watched. He crooned in my ear, "Trust Daddy, baby. you know I am only going to do what is best for you, right?"

I nodded my head in response.

"No tears then, My little one. you never know what may happen while the procedure is being done." Daddy winked at me as he straightened up and told David that he understood.

David went on. "You will have to arouse her with your fingers or a toy. I can't have any semen or saliva on her genitals."

Again, Daddy nodded.

David continued, "And you know she has to be completely still during the procedure. You have requested we not use any local anesthesia during the procedure. I have no problem with that. We'll go with the plan we discussed for keeping her still." he grinned.

*Plan? What plan?*

"I have one last offer for you, Kane. Let my staff and I watch you arouse her and let my assistants watch the piercing and I'll give you a twenty percent discount. I have an assistant who has never done one of these and he needs to watch. Usually, we give the couple privacy for the arousal, but you indicated it wasn't necessary."

Daddy nodded, saying, "Now *that* I will agree to; everyone can watch, no problem."

I was extremely aroused at the thought of everyone watching. It wasn't exactly what I had in mind, but it was a start.

David called to his staff to put out the "Gone to Lunch" sign, lock the door, and come on back to watch and learn. Within two minutes, both men were in the small room. David rolled back up to my crotch and snapped on latex gloves.

The two new guys leaned over me as David's rough fingers gently handled my lips.

"Okay, guys, this lady is here to have her clitoral hood pierced." Instantly, a bit of relief washed over me as I realized Daddy didn't intend to have my actual clit pierced. I got warm over the mind fuck Daddy pulled on me, and giggled at the possibility of what was to come.

David continued the lesson. "She has long inner labia that will also be pierced with small gold rings. Kane will arouse her before we begin, so that her clit is fully swollen. That will ensure the piercing does not interfere with her arousal in the future. If I pierced the hood while she was not aroused, then the piercing might interfere with her clit swelling later and cause her pain. Now, some guys want that, but not this time. Kane will also be the one to hold her while I do the piercing. Remember, I told you about the 'technique' he plans to use."

I raised my head and looked at the men around the room and saw all of their trousers tented out. I felt my arousal growing. In a perfect fantasy scenario, I would have them all coming on my breasts while the procedure was being done, since I needed to stay aroused during the procedure. But to admit that to Daddy and have him oblige me would have been a gross breach of House protocol and a punishment I wouldn't have been able to bear. So, I kept my mouth shut in anticipation of how he would keep me stimulated.

David ran a gloved finger down my wet open slit. "It shouldn't be any problem to get her aroused. I think she likes all of this attention." David grinned at the lewd and lascivious atmosphere we'd created for this appointment. "Okay, Kane, we'll wait right here until you have her ready and still."

Daddy pulled me up and pulled my feet out of the stirrups. I sat up straight and he helped me off the table. He sat down in an armless chair across from our audience. He guided me to stand between his legs. He buried his face into my stomach, slid his hands up to cup my breasts. He lingered there for a minute fingering my hard tight nipples. God, *it felt so good* to feel his touch again. Then he let his hands slide up to my shoulders and pushed down slightly.

I remembered that signal well. I quickly knelt between his legs. He cupped my chin and looked into my eyes. "shamise."

I barely whispered, "Yes, Daddy."

"Who do you belong to?"

"my mind, body, and heart belong to You and my Goddess."

"Good girl."

Tears welled up in my eyes. I was ashamed of disappointing him, either of them. My leaving the family that loved me had disappointed them both, and the reality of the situation finally hit me.

He continued, "I am proud of you for not trying to stop Me and for not saying anything. So, your spanking won't be too bad." My eyes tried not to betray my shock at his intention to spank me in front of an audience. "Now, take out My dick."

I couldn't get the pants unzipped fast enough.

Without any underwear, his member sprang up, thick and hard and oozing at the tip. I looked at it longingly, remembering every detail all over again.

He chuckled. "Yes, baby, you may have a taste."

I dove in, licking and sucking his shaft, one hand grasping it by the base. My other hand scooped under his balls to caress them. He leaned back to enjoy the sight and feel. I watched out of the corner of my eye at the other men in the room rubbing the bulges in their pants. One by one, they opened their trousers to let their hard swollen cocks free. Each man stroked his own stiff dick.

"Lap," Daddy commanded.

I lay across his lap and he swiveled his chair so my shapely ass was facing our audience.

"Spread."

He nudged my legs far apart and ran his hands slowly over my cool, caramel ass cheeks.

One of the men in the room spoke up, "Damn, look at the ass on that bitch."

"Wait until you see it red and glowing. It's even prettier then." He let his fingers trail down the crack of my ass to my dripping pussy.

He brought his hand up and began to pat my ass at first, alternating with rubbing. I moaned in my continuing arousal. Slowly, he began to spank me harder. It happened so gradually I didn't feel any real pain, only intense arousal. The sting of his smacks intensified my desire for him, the tingle in my pussy, and the swelling of my clit.

Between smacks, he caressed my soaking wet lips and let his index finger slide down to my clit; it was hard and throbbing and so swollen. I guess Daddy decided it was time to get more serious and began to rain harder slaps down on my ass. Then he let a blow strike my sensitive pussy.

That slap raised my head and I let out a scream, then let my head drop and I moaned some more.

"Oh my God, she's so sexy. I'm gonna come." The youngest guy in the room could no longer hold back. I heard him groaning and imagined the semen spurting from his shaft as he slumped against the wall.

Daddy's blows came harder with one landing on my pussy every now and then. I felt myself flowing into space with each strike across my ass. He paused to feel my clit and found it more swollen than he could ever remember. I was desperately trying to ignore his stiffness pushing into my stomach. I could feel the slippery tip smearing pre-come all over me. Harder blows rained down on my hot ass, which I knew had begun to glow red. He let every third blow land on my pussy.

I was moaning loudly now, my ass instinctively rising up to meet every blow. He was spanking me like a man possessed.

My body was beginning to betray me, tears flowing freely now. For quite a few blows, he didn't let up. I began to babble, *"Sir… Sir…Sir…"*

Without stopping his smacking, he asked, "What, baby? What do you need?"

I went limp on his lap and burst out, *"RED!"*

He knew he had given me all that I could take.

He rubbed his hand over my ass. It felt so hot. He leaned over and looked between my widely spread legs. From his fingertips, I felt my sex pulsating and my clit protruded from its hood. I felt it pulse with every beat of my heart as Daddy pressed against it.

I was at the point of no return, and I became the wanton slut he'd wanted to awaken from within. I raised my head and looked over my shoulder at him. "Fuck me, please, fuck me, Daddy! Please fuck me! I need to be fucked! Please put Your dick in me and fuck me!"

We caught a movement out of the corner of his eye. My words

and screams had finally put David over the edge. I briefly watched David's come shoot into the air, giggling at the thought I'd put two men into orgasmic bliss without touching either one.

Daddy reached to the counter beside him and picked up a bottle of lubricant. I hadn't seen him put it there, but I was too far gone to care where it came from. All other thoughts were driven from my head as I felt the cold lubricant dripped onto my tightly clenched asshole.

God I loved what I knew would come next.

His finger probed my asshole, spreading the lubricant and loosening me up. "Relax that ass for Me."

Daddy slowly twisted his finger in my asshole to spread the lubricant all the way around. With his other hand, he dribbled a few more drops onto me.

He began to plunge his finger in and out of my tight asshole, dripping more lubricant and letting a second finger slide inside. He was mesmerized by the sight of his fingers sliding in and out of my ass. I swear I could have come all over the place right then. He watched the sphincter stretch to accommodate his fingers, but it was as tight as a vise. He continued dipping his two fingers in and out a few more times as his engorged member throbbed intensely, impatiently waiting its turn to slide inside me.

He realized I was mumbling something. "What did you say, baby?"

I lifted my head. "*PLEASE* fuck me, Daddy!"

He grinned and let a last couple of drops of lubricant drip onto my asshole. He was pleased to see when he removed his fingers that my ass didn't clench back shut as tightly. I was proud of that, too, and refused to hide my lustful grin.

He urged me up and as I got to my feet, he quickly rubbed a gob of lubricant down his shaft. He hastily wiped his hand on a paper towel from a dispenser on the wall, fortunately within easy reach. Daddy's slut was practically in a trance, my arousal at an all-time high. He knew the spanking would do this to me, and I didn't care anymore. I belonged to him. At this point, I would've done absolutely anything he wanted without question or embarrassment. He grasped my hips and turned me around with my back to him; my face to the three guys a few feet away across the small room.

Daddy's shaft pointed straight up in his lap. He slowly lowered my reddened ass down until the tip of his dick was touching it. He put one hand on my hip and adjusted my stance until he was perfectly aligned with my asshole. He grasped his thickness with one hand and urged me down with his other hand on my hip.

At first, I tried to clench against his invasion of my chocolate hole, but he persisted and he felt it finally give way as I pressed my weight against him. I had waited so long for this, I'd completely forgotten what we were really there for. Inch by inch, I slid down, moaning and whimpering, taking him into me completely.

Daddy encouraged me. "Yes, baby, open up for Me. Take it all in, baby. You know you can take it all. You know your ass needs fucking. You know you want this."

Daddy was always fascinated by the sight of his dick sliding into my ass. I heard him cursing at how good it felt. The skin around my asshole stretched so taut it turned white. I wondered at its ability to stretch around his swollen cock without splitting. Daddy wondered why I didn't scream in pain whenever he fucked me. That part was easy. I loved it when he fucked me anally. Then I remembered what a powerful anesthetic my arousal was. At that moment, I could not feel any pain.

I slid the last inch until his length was completely embedded inside me. I sat on Daddy's lap, my back leaning into him, impaled by his rod in my ass. He gritted his teeth and willed his ejaculation away for the moment. He reached around me and pulled my legs up over his, so my legs were on the outside of his. Then he spread his legs until mine were spread as widely as possible.

He wrapped his arms around me and held me close; a hand covering each breast, his fingers on my hard nipples. He glanced across at David and nodded. David had recovered from his ejaculation and tucked his limp dick back into his pants. He quickly snapped on fresh latex gloves and rolled his chair forward; a tray of sterile implements on his lap.

My head was thrown back and resting on Daddy's shoulder. My ass squeezed his dick; my arms limply by my sides, almost completely zoned out. He spoke in my ear, "shamise, I think it will be sooo sexy to see you pierced. I'm going to let David pierce you now. Do you want that, baby?"

My head rolled slightly and I murmured, "Yes, Daddy, I want that. I want anything You want."

He nodded at David again. David delicately pulled the hood up from my swollen throbbing clit and quickly punched the needle through. Daddy held me tightly, afraid I might jerk, even though I couldn't really move much with his dick up my ass. But he was surprised when I didn't jerk, but moaned and squeezed his dick even tighter with the muscles of my ass.

I began to beg him, eyes closed, head still back on his shoulder. "Please make me come, Daddy; please, can i come?!?!?!"

David was grinning, awed by the sight of how my clit had swollen and reddened. They both knew that I was teetering on the edge of orgasm. David was careful not to touch my clit any more than absolutely necessary, per Daddy's instructions. The needle slid through the slack skin, dragging a gold bar through the new opening.

Daddy spoke in my ear, "Not yet, baby, let's get that pussy all decorated first. you are *NOT* allowed to come yet, little one. Be a good girl and wait. Just concentrate on My dick in your ass."

I moaned and rolled my head and began rhythmically squeezing his dick, feeling it consuming me, inching deeper.

David could see the sphincter contracting and releasing. He felt his own soldier rising for battle again.

David turned to gesture his assistants closer to see his work, but both of them were leaning against the wall, dicks in hand again. Sighing, David picked up new implements and began on my pussy lips. First, he gently pulled them both out together and carefully marked each side. He wanted them to be even. Then one at a time, he pulled the lips out to pierce them.

As the needle slid easily through the first inner lip, I moaned and cried out, "Oh my God, Daddy; I need to *COME* so badly, please???"

Desperately trying to hold his own orgasm against my squeezing, Daddy gritted his teeth and managed to growl softly, "No, baby, not yet; soon I promise, soon, but not yet."

David pulled out the other inner lip and deftly pushed the needle through it. I moaned and begged more desperately, *"Oh please, Daddy, please let me come!!!"*

David knew I was so close, so he needed to work fast. He was throbbing with desperation and needed to release.

Daddy managed to calm me down again before I slipped over the edge of orgasm. "Focus on My dick, baby; you know that is your first priority." He wanted to tell me to wait until HE came, but his own control was so tenuous he was afraid he would spurt prematurely.

David adjusted his hardness in his pants. He vowed to free it and join his coworkers in masturbating again as soon as he was finished. He glanced over his shoulder and saw his staff panting, rubbing their members up and down, and staring wide-eyed at the erotic sight before them. David had to admit this was the most erotic piercing he had ever done. Never before had he pierced a woman while she was impaled.

Deftly, he slipped the tiny gold rings into place, first one and then the other. He realized he was sweating as he rolled his chair back and nodded to Daddy. David whipped him out, perilously close to coming in his pants. Daddy relaxed a tiny bit and snaked his hand around to my obscenely spread crotch. He fingered the gold bar through the hood of my clit and then the tiny gold rings dangling from my outer lips.

Smiling with satisfaction, he spoke in my ear again, "Okay, baby, when you make Me come, you can come with Me." Held tightly on his lap, I squirmed and squeezed. He rubbed his finger over my wet slit to lubricate it and then planted it squarely over my throbbing clit.

I cried out, "Daddy, please fill me! Please come deep in my ass!" I squeezed and bounced as I screamed.

For one last desperate second, he held out, feeling the hot slippery vise massaging his rigid girth. Then with a warning, he erupted. "Yes, baby, I'm gonna fill you up! *I'm coming!*"

His body jerked as each stream of thick cream pumped into my ass. I bucked wildly on his lap, engrossed in my own orgasm. I was screaming his name and nearly crying with the intense release. He managed to keep his finger pressing and rubbing my clit, his other hand around my waist holding me tightly. He didn't let up on rubbing my throbbing clit until I collapsed back against his chest, panting and letting myself burst into tears.

He held me tightly still, his free hand caressing me, soothing me. He kissed me softly on the nape of my neck and murmured how very much he loved me; how much my Goddess adored me and how much my sis idolized me. Relaxed from the release I had craved so badly, I finally opened my eyes. I could feel him shrinking inside me. I picked up my head and giggled. He followed my gaze to where the three men were sprawled, their swollen pieces still in hand. Their hands were covered in sticky gooey semen.

He gently bit my earlobe and whispered, "Look at what you did to those men! I think you have earned yourself another spanking tonight!" I lifted my eyebrows and smiled at the thought. He lifted me carefully and we both paused while we felt his limp, slippery shaft slide out of my ass.

He stood up and bent me over the chair, ass toward the men watching. He told me to spread my legs. My own juices ran in rivulets down the inside of my thighs. He parted my ass cheeks and they all watched fascinated as gobs of thick white semen oozed from my asshole, which gaped slightly from the fucking. He rubbed his hands over my still-red warm ass. He glanced at the men leering at me. "Now, that, gentlemen, is how a woman's ass should look after it's been used."

He commanded me to pick up my clothes and to redress. The extra guys, realizing the show was over, returned to their work. David mumbled as he left, "I'll meet you at the counter." I would have sworn he sounded a bit disappointed about the whole thing being over so soon. While the actual procedure lasted maybe ten minutes, getting me "there" took damn near twenty. It was a long time to be that stimulated, but I was used to it. In the past, Daddy had me in heat for at least twelve hours, constantly on the edge and back.

Before Daddy let me put on my skirt, he stood me in front of the mirror on the back of the door and spread my legs to look at the piercings.

"How do you like it, My little one?" he asked.

I blushed. "I think it is pretty, but mostly i am glad that it pleases You, Daddy."

He pulled up my skirt and I slid my feet into my sandals. He hugged me tightly, which I admit made me feel completely consumed because of his sheer size and height. "It pleases Me very much, baby."

"Thank You, my Pharaoh." My body shook, still enjoying the encompassing feeling of his embrace. God, he made me feel so safe. "It is my desire to please You always."

He led me out to the counter to pay their bill. My ass and thighs were still wet from my juices, but I knew he would never let me wipe it off and he hadn't given me time or permission to massage it in. The men worked halfheartedly, but stopped when I appeared. They watched my ass, barely covered by the skirt, and watched the semen still trickling down my legs.

David pushed an invoice over the counter. Daddy pulled out his wallet as he looked over the bill. "David, this is more of a discount than we agreed on," he noticed.

David smiled slowly and responded, "Well, Kane, that was quite a show. The guys and I enjoyed it far too much to charge you what we agreed on."

Daddy smiled, paid the bill, and left a generous tip.

"Come again, soon!" David called out as we walked out the door.

Daddy grinned at me, causing me to blush again. He turned to David and said, "If she's a good girl, this sexy little one's sister will be coming…and *very* soon!"

# TWENTY-ONE ⊗ SHAMISE

I was still on a sexual high from my new piercing.

Fuck, it hurt, but it felt so fucking good, and to top it off, to know that I was one step closer to being back where I belonged only added to the high I was on.

I guess that's why I didn't flip out when I stumbled onto a scene I didn't expect to be an unwitting party to.

"Damn, tiger, you're doing a better job than the masseuse i see on a weekly basis. Keep this up and i might have to pay you what i pay her."

"Oh, flattery will get you everywhere, sexy. i don't know why you keep flexing like you don't like my hands on you."

Ice was on tiger's massage table, getting a naked rubdown that definitely did not look like an innocent massage and talk between them. Damn, I forgot how fuckable Ice was, and it had been a while since we'd been intimate, but that was a different time back then. I belonged to Daddy and Goddess and I was given permission to "have" Ice during a swing party they hosted at the House. Damn, he was so…insatiable…I had to beg to take a break so I could catch my breath.

Now, things have changed, especially the way he'd been acting as of lately. He had been a jackass, and that's putting it mildly. The past few weeks in particular had been unbearable to deal with him.

He kept trying to fuck me at every opportunity, all the while trying his best to act like his wife repulsed him.

Despite my disdain for him and the way he'd been treating both my sis and me, my body betrayed me on levels I didn't have a clue about. I hated feeling the wetness between my legs, trying to trick my mind into believing that he wasn't the cause of it, ignoring the fact that I was attracted to a beautiful male body. Ice was beautiful; there was no denying it.

The other thing I couldn't deny was what was transpiring in front of me.

I watched as tiger grabbed more massage oil and worked on Ice's calves, moving up to the back of his thighs. He slid his hands over Ice's ass, and I expected him to flinch and tell tiger to move his hands, but he didn't.

I was confused by his lack of reaction. Ice never struck me as being flexible with his sexuality like that. But the more tiger massaged his ass and the inside of his thighs, the more Ice moaned and groaned like he *wanted* tiger to keep going.

"Okay, time for the front." Ice flipped over, and I was shocked to see his manhood was rock-hard and standing at full attention. He moved over Ice's chest first, working his way down to his stomach; all the while I saw his hips bucking upward, almost begging for more intimate attention from tiger. When tiger's hand slid across the tip of his shaft, Ice still didn't flinch.

"Sorry, bro."

"Don't worry about it, bro. i always get hard when i get a massage. My body doesn't tell the difference between a man touching me or a woman touching me. Is that weird?"

"Dude, you're asking the wrong person; i'm good with both teams, remember?" tiger moved down to his legs and I noticed Ice close his eyes, getting more comfortable as tiger continued to massage his thighs.

I felt like I was betraying some privacy rule or something. I was a guest in his home. Yes, I was a guest by his wife's invitation, but I still felt like I was intruding on something I shouldn't have been. At the same time, he was allowing someone else to touch him… to handle his dick…in a manner that didn't seem, well, right. I don't mean right like "he's not supposed to be gay" right; I was more along the lines of "your wife doesn't know you're doing shit like this" right.

But that's not entirely accurate, either. tiger had told sajira that they had been intimate, but for this to be happening under her own roof? He was blurring the lines and that wasn't cool at all. All he had to do was come clean and let his wife make an informed decision as to how to proceed.

Bastard…I should kill his vibe and then some!

I decided to let the scene play itself out, if for nothing else than for blackmailing purposes and masturbatory purposes. Watching two men getting together was hot as fuck to me, and I wasn't about to interrupt this for anything. I was, however, going to blow up his spot thinking he could get away with doing this shit to his wife without at least coming clean about it.

tiger had his hands around Ice's engorged member and poured oil all over his hand as it squeezed it tighter.

"Oh, fuck, that feels good."

"Good boi, i'm glad you're enjoying yourself. i've been wanting to do this for a while, you know?"

"Mmmm, yeah, i know. To be honest, i've been curious about what it might feel like to, well, you know."

"Say it, Ice."

He hesitated for a moment. His eyes were still closed as I imagined he contemplated his answer. "I…I want to know what it's like for you to suck my dick."

tiger continued to stroke Ice, torturing him. "Beg me."

"Suck my dick, tiger, please."

I tried to hold my gasps and moans in as I continued to take the scene in. My mind wanted to stop it before it really got out of control, but my body kept responding; my nipples were so hard they began to hurt and squeezing my thighs together only made things worse. The pressure shot through my clit, and I bit my lip harder to keep from screaming out.

tiger bent down, his tongue licking the head, licking his entire length, treating his dick like it was a chocolate ice cream cone, closing his eyes and getting into a zone as he began to piston up and down, clamping down and creating the suction he needed to make his mouth feel like a pussy squeezing tight. Ice gripped the back of tiger's head, arching his back in a futile fight for control of his pleasure. Watching him writhing and trying to keep from groaning and screaming, they had me turned on to no end.

His hips lifted completely off the table, yelling at the top of his lungs that he was coming. tiger never stopped sucking; he never lifted to let him spurt on his hands or anything like that; he drank everything down like it was his favorite milkshake.

"Damn, that was amazing." Ice lifted up and kissed him deeply, causing me to cover my mouth with my hand to keep from shouting. *No, this son of a bitch did not do what I thought he did?*

I walked away from the room, in desperate need to get away from the scene as my mind began to override my body at that point. The last words I heard out of tiger's mouth before I disappeared upstairs were, "Get on the bed, bitch; i'm about to take that ass now."

Yeah, I was definitely going to blow his mind when he got done before my sis arrived home. He needs to be set straight on some things as soon as possible before he fucks up on biblical levels.

⚜

"Fuck, you scared the devil out of me, woman; what the fuck is wrong with you?"

Flipping on the light switch to the kitchen and unexpectedly seeing me waiting on him as he walked to get a bottled water out of the fridge, the menacing stare that greeted him temporarily caused him to forget about the fleeting moment of fear, thinking that there was someone he didn't recognize in his home.

"i should ask you the same question, dude," I retorted. My arms were folded across my chest, completely closed off with an "I wish you would" look that let him know this was not going to be one of those easy days, at least, not for him. "What the fuck is wrong with you?"

"i don't know what you're talking about."

"Yes the fuck you do, you stupid jackass."

"Oh, we're resorting to name calling now?"

"We are when we got busted having a man suck our dick when anyone could have come home and seen it all happen."

Ice froze. "you didn't see shit."

"i believe the proper words were, 'get on the bed, bitch; i'm about to take that ass now,' right?"

"It wasn't what you think it...tiger—"

"Has been wanting to suck and fuck you for a while now, yeah, i know." I didn't have time for the bullshit. I was beyond the point of worrying about what my supposed "lying eyes" might or might not have seen. "The funny thing is, he told me he was gonna fuck you, and i told him you weren't that stupid to fall for it. i guess the joke's on me, huh?"

Ice had the nerve to look pissed. "So, what are you gonna do, huh? Are you gonna drop a dime on my wife?"

"No, you should have come clean a long time ago, dumb ass." I was so pissed I could have taken a piece of steel and knocked him upside his head. "If you don't come clean to her, and i mean as soon as fucking possible, you'll leave me no choice but to fuck up your whole world, and that means your Mistress, too."

"you wouldn't…"

"Oh, wouldn't i? Have you forgotten the clout i have with the Dominants in the community? i have taken great pains to make sure my word, my recollections of how things happen are exactly what happened." I stared him down, never once flinching or moving a muscle in the chair. "your Mistress knows i have no reason to lie, and if i recall correctly, you're not exactly in Her good graces at the current moment. A transgression like this is likely to really have your ass in a sling."

His eyes widened. Leave it to a punk like him to fear the punishment of his Mistress more than the pain of divorce. "Scarlett, we can work something out; i can't be in trouble again. The punishment would be too great."

"you know what? That information made my decision that much easier to make." I watched him squirm while I let the decision roll around in my head a few times. He was lucky I had more love for my sis than I had contempt for watching him suffer. "you have until after her collaring ceremony to let her know what's going on. i would say before, but i don't want anything fucking up my sis's collaring, not even your bitch ass."

Ice put his head in his hands, his shoulders slumping like he'd been through the fight of his life. "Look, i didn't want things to go down like this; you have to believe me."

"Well, you have a fucked-up way of expressing your sorrow." I reverted to the scene of the two of them in my head, shaking my head at the mixed emotions I felt. My Goddess would have loved to direct the scene between them, and if tiger got his way earlier, I would have taken great pleasure in watching him on all fours, taking the dick as well, if not better, than any women he'd been with before he married sajira. "The clock is ticking, bitch. Figure out how you're going to tell her, or it won't be pleasant."

# TWENTY-TWO ⊗ RAMESSES

*No nerves. This is a routine trip, nothing more.*

That's what I repeated to myself.

As much as I wanted to say I wouldn't be nervous, or not let every single detail get to me or throw me off balance, the fact remained: I had every reason to be nervous.

I was in the midst of leading a contingent of the majority of the members of *Neb'net Maa'kheru*, including Amenhotep, around the grounds of NEBU, rattling off all of the changes made to the compound. Neferterri stayed in the main building with sajira and shamise to oversee the NEBU slaves as they prepared dinner upon our return from the tour.

My mentor smiled at seeing all of the changes up close and personal, and while it made me smile on the outside to know he was pleased with the upgrades and changes, it wasn't the reason why my nerves were on edge.

Seti had not arrived to NEBU yet.

My emotions were conflicted. Before nadia took me back to the airport, Seti made sure to inform me he would be in Atlanta in time for the meeting of the members to tour the facility. In fact, one of the service slaves had confirmed the limousine had been sent to pick up his entourage from Hartsfield-Jackson. It was my sole purpose for allowing the advanced viewing. Otherwise, it would have only been Dominic, Amenhotep and me set to tour.

I had a feeling Seti was testing my patience for a reason, especially when he had prior knowledge his brother would be in attendance.

I'll be damned if I was going to be disrespected in my own backyard.

I watched Amenhotep's facial expressions and the different range of emotions that gave me everything I needed to know concerning whether I had done well or not. His eyes met mine, and a knowing wink from Him was confirmation that all the stressing I had put myself through while getting everything put together was well worth the effort.

I didn't feel so burdened anymore. It was almost like the monkey was finally off my back, even though I was the one who put it there.

"It seems You have done quite well with the design and construction of the grounds, Ramesses," Master Menes remarked as we stepped out of the touring cart and began to make our way into the main building. "I am quite looking forward to seeing how things will work out at the future compounds."

"Yes, I agree with Menes," Osiris chimed in, strolling beside me as we reached the stairs to the front entrance. "I am pleased I agreed to begin construction in the Vegas area. I believe the California contingent would be very excited to see this as well. I am hoping You have done a visual markup of the grounds so we can take this to some of the more influential community members and wow them as You have wowed us here today."

"Yes, Sir, I have had that done, both aerial and on the grounds, Osiris." I caught one of the NEBU slaves trying to get my attention. I dismissed her for the moment, concentrating on Seti's absence instead. "I had hoped I would have shown Your brother the grounds also, but it seems He has been delayed to some degree."

I had a strange feeling I should have excused myself from the group when the NEBU slave risked breaking protocol to warn me about something. But that no longer mattered as a small contingent approached us, and upon seeing slave nadia leading the contingent, I almost wished I had allowed the breach of protocol.

Seti had emerged, looking perturbed like he had been waiting an extraordinarily long time for the group to return so he could give everyone an earful, specifically me.

"Ramesses, may I ask why You took the group on a tour of the grounds without including Me?" He stared me down as he spoke. The moment he stepped into my personal space, my guard was heightened. "Surely You of all people should know better than to leave a member of the Order in the lurch."

Amenhotep replied to Seti before I could interject. "You made it a point to keep the rest of the members waiting, Seti. Unless I missed My guess, we were all scheduled to meet at three p.m. sharp so Ramesses could begin the tour," He made mention as He looked at His watch. "We did not begin the tour until nearly three-thirty, and You had not left word, nor did You instruct any of Your slaves to do so, which leads the rest of the members to believe Your lack of punctuality was a deliberate act. Do You not have the other members' cell phone numbers?"

Seti tried to dismiss Amenhotep's reply, which infuriated me. His eyes never left mine when he said, "Amenhotep, I do not remember asking You the question that I posed to Ramesses. I believe He can speak for Himself."

In my mind I yelled a plethora of profanities, but I needed to keep my emotions in check, especially around Seti. There were too many in attendance, and the last thing I needed was to have an incident happen to get back to the blog boards and get blown out of proportion. It was only a matter of time before he tried to say something else to enrage me, and the attack would be warranted.

Thankfully, Osiris began his assault before I could get started.

"Seti, what exactly is the issue, besides Your ability to try and place the spotlight on You?" Osiris asked of his brother, equally irritated at his dispassionate demeanor. "If You are insistent upon continuing this longstanding grudge between You and Me, then the least You can do is leave the rest of the members out of it and conduct Yourself with the decorum expectant of a member of *Neb'net Maa'kheru.*"

"You are the last person to educate Me on decorum, *brother.*" Seti looked nearly insulted Osiris would even speak to him in any tone at all. "You were the one to break decorum and protocol when You deliberately took Your current slave from Me."

"You seem to want to distort the facts of the matter from that time, *brother.*" Osiris bellowed loud enough to snap everyone's attention in our direction. "Do You really insist on putting things out there while thinking You were in the right?"

"I was in the right!" Seti yelled.

Osiris didn't want to bring this issue out in the open, not exactly in this manner, and certainly not in front of the current slaves at Seti's feet, witnessing the standoff between blood. I shook my head, realizing I was privy to the information that was about to become public record in my compound.

"Since You insist, so be it. Do You recall when You broke Your House protocol, at My insistence You do not for Your own benefit, that led to Your former, slave leticia, to request and secure release from Your control?" Osiris inquired while the audience had his attention. He swept his eyes across the faces around him, much like a prosecutor looking to sway the jury with his argument.

That question nearly stopped Seti dead in his tracks. From the history I remembered during the conversations with both Amenhotep and Osiris, the former slave leticia was now the current slave keket. The confused look on Seti's face gave his brother the upper hand, and without a rebuttal worth speaking, he left the door wide open to have the rest of that history dropped at the feet of everyone within earshot, regardless of station.

Osiris kept up his onslaught. "I see from Your expression that You do remember. I also recall putting My own status within the Society at risk because according to the bylaws, the actions You caused would have led to Your censure and removal from the Society. I kept You from being removed, under the promise that neither of us would speak of it, *ever*, until You forced Me to do so now."

keket stood close to her Master, finding a spot on his upper back.

*"You still had no right to accept leticia as one of Your own!"* Seti had become irate by that point, as the memories flooded back to him like a raging tsunami. *"she had no business even being with You; You were My brother, dammit!"*

*"All right, that's enough!"* I had to put a stop to this now before any more damage would be done. "I may not be a member of the Society, but I can no longer stand idly by and allow this feud to continue."

"Ramesses, this is none of Your—" Seti tried to back me off, but saw a look in my eyes that let him know that I would not be denied, not this time.

"Oh, but I believe it is *MY* affair now, Master Seti," I retorted. "You see, Sir, the bylaws of this and the other compounds clearly stipulate any discourse is to be arbitrated by the Head of Council of the compound the discourse or dispute occurs in. Now, while You are Head of Council at *Thebes*, and Osiris is Head of Council at

*Deshret*, I am the Head of Council here at NEBU. When any Head of Council is at a visiting compound, they must yield to the host Head of Council, which means You *will* yield, or be removed not only from the grounds, but from Your position as Head of Council at *Thebes* also. My question to You, Master Seti: do You yield?"

The line was drawn in the sand.

Seti's anger was evident on his face, and his anger was matched by the determination in my face and the perseverance to ensure time stopped and nothing else would be done until this issue was resolved.

He stared into my eyes once again, in search of something that no longer existed. My stare into his eyes posed a rhetorical question: do you really want things to end like this?

To say the group was so quiet you could only hear the rustle of the wind in the trees would be an understatement. Despite the way I looked, the urge to back down reared its ugly head. This was high-stakes poker, and the last one who blinked had the advantage. I cut a quick glance at Amenhotep, who simply nodded in response to my silent plea of whether or not I had crossed the line to restore order.

Neferterri, sajira and shamise had been told by the NEBU slaves something was wrong and saw the tail end of the exchange between Seti and Osiris and my interruption of the two of them. I saw them out of the corner of my eye and slowly raised a hand to stop them from interfering. This was something I needed to do, and any outside influences would ruin the momentum I'd built.

It might have looked like a pissing contest, and to a degree, it probably was. But this was how Alpha males, no, Dominant males, took care of business, without the added escalation to violence, although if it had to go there, then it had to go there. Honor and respect were earned, not given, and I was going to earn mine from Seti, even if I had to resort to dropping him like a ton of bricks to get it.

Finally, Seti spoke. "Lord Ramesses, I will yield as stipulated by the bylaws of NEBU. I apologize for causing this scene to occur, and I would like to offer the ability to speak with My brother, with You as arbiter, to bring this feud to an end once and for all. The Society is bigger than the two of us, and we've strayed from that ideal."

"I will concede to this meeting also, Lord Ramesses." Osiris put a hand on my shoulder in an attempt to diffuse the situation and restore a sense of calm to what was a successful group outing. "This has been a long time coming, but the egos and stubbornness of two old fools would not allow it. I believe things will finally be at peace after all these years."

"Very good, then, gentlemen, I believe we can accommodate this immediately." I finally found the words to say, although I really felt I should never have stepped out of place. I knew I would deal with those actions when Amenhotep and I spoke in private. "I believe that settles things."

The NEBU slave, still in her kneeling position during the entire exchange, kissed the back of my palm, alerting me to her presence. Upon looking down and acknowledging her to speak, she stated, "m'Lord, dinner is prepared. When You and Your party are ready, we would be at Your disposal to serve dinner."

"Very good, My dear." I dismissed her to join the others in the kitchen to prepare to serve dinner, turning my attention back to the group. "Now, I invite You all to move to the dining room, please, so the slaves may serve dinner."

☥

"I understand if I overstepped My place, Sir."

I wasn't up to eating at the moment. I was more concerned about my less than honorable actions a few minutes earlier.

"Kid, I think if You trust Your instincts, You would have pretty much figured I'm not upset about You standing Your ground and stepping into the fray between Osiris and Seti. The silence You heard was the admiration of someone growing up." Amenhotep smiled, sitting down in a chair within a side room not far from the dining room.

"But, Sir, I am not a member of the Order. It was not My place to interfere," I protested, almost feeling like I was begging to be punished for a crime I knew I'd committed. "There's no way I should have been allowed, Sir."

"I believe Seti would have been more than happy to agree with You. Hell, He was set on nearly reminding You of that fact. And yet, it was You who had the strength of will and conviction, and the foresight to write the clause into the bylaws, for just such an occasion," Amenhotep reminded me. "Those two sons of bitches are coming to some sort of accord, thanks to You. I don't think they're going to worry about the bylaws of the Order now, especially when what Osiris said was correct, for the most part."

"You mean, Seti would have been censured and removed?" I queried.

"Yes, but because the events they had spoken of occurred beyond the calendar year statute of limitations for any egregious acts, the only thing Osiris accomplished was to help bring focus to and provide You the opening to lower the boom on Seti."

"Wait a minute; Seti had to know about that part of the clause in the bylaws," I countered, trying to collect my thoughts. Something didn't sound right. "I thought He was the one who was a stickler for the rules."

"Seti is not as thorough as He would lead You to believe, kid," Amenhotep said. "In fact, if He had been, this would have been resolved eons ago. He chose to forget about the minute details in favor of keeping his grudge. He'd been pissed for so long, He'd forgotten to check the bylaws to make sure He was still in the right."

"So, what happens now, Sir, do I just simply act like nothing has happened, or what?"

"I don't know about You, youngster, but I am going to enjoy My dinner, since the girls have so lovingly prepared things for our arrival," Amenhotep told me. He winked, giving me the clue that He was going to enjoy the rest of His evening, with or without me.

"All right, Sir, I'll put whatever thoughts I have out of My mind and worry about it another time. For now, there is some celebrating that must be done."

I honestly still felt I'd done something wrong, but it was no longer for me to judge. Besides, I didn't have the benefit of reading and understanding the bylaws within the Society, so I couldn't say for certain if I did or did not act in error. I did act righteously as Head of Council, however, but I felt like I'd copped out.

That's a guilt trip for another day.

One thing was for certain: this was going to be one celebration and grand reopening that would be remembered for a long time.

# TWENTY-THREE ⚸ SAJIRA

"Wow! I hardly recognize the place."

I laughed at the reactions of the contingent that was with me to tour the grounds. Sinsual, Blaze, Ethereal, the bois, shamise and sajira, all took in the splendor that millions of dollars took care of and cultivated. Once Ramesses was done with the drama that had happened earlier, it gave me the opportunity to show the place off in my own way. He was more interested in showing off the nuts-and-bolts, but we women are a bit more nuanced when it comes to really showing off a place.

I admit, though, if I wasn't with my Beloved during the final phases of construction, I would have reacted the same way they did.

Simply put, NEBU looked *nothing* like the old Palace grounds.

Outside of the main building, the acreage had been put to its full potential. Every possible area and corner had been meticulously landscaped to give the patrons an experience like any other. They marveled at the cobblestone walkways that separated the houses. Instead of electrical lamps, glass-blown oil lamps adorned the walkways, adding to the ambiance. It was quiet and intimate, despite the size of the property and the number of houses on the grounds. Amenhotep and Ramesses had broken the bank to transform this place. Why He hadn't done this in the first place I'd never understand.

"This place looks like we're in another world," Sin mentioned as she looked at yet another house we walked past, taking us deeper into the edges of the property. "When Your husband wants to do it big...I'm still in awe."

"Are You sure we're still in Atlanta?" Blaze asked. "The way this is set up, you would think we took a trip out of the country or something."

"Ladies, all I can say is enjoy it while it lasts," I remarked. While the extra properties added some significant value to the land, it was going to take some creative marketing to keep this place solvent. Call it the accountant in me, but it still took money to make money. "I know they have big plans for the times and days that we aren't operating on the weekends. It's going to be busy, and if you want to still be on the ground floor with this, it's going to take some effort."

"Well, once word gets out about this place, a lot of the other dungeon owners are gonna be really worried and ready to throw some shade on this place," Sin stated. "I hope it does last, but I'm going to enjoy Myself tonight."

"I'm sure they will try, but knowing Ramesses, He loves getting ahead of drama," Ethereal said. She continued to enjoy the interior design of the houses. "Have they figured out the pricing to work things out for folks that might not exactly 'afford' this place?"

"According to Amenhotep, He wanted to make sure that no one had to take out any personal loans to enjoy things," I explained. "But I have a feeling there will be other ways this place will make money. I know My husband too well."

"What I wanna know is whether or not we will get a chance to do something special. You think, like something for the Dominas. Maybe a conference type of set-up?" Blaze asked. I saw the other ladies' eyes light up, and it sparked an idea inside my mind.

"Goddess, if i may suggest something?" shamise waited for my nod before continuing with her thought. "i believe a pseudo-Samois conference would be a very good idea. It hasn't really been done, at least on the scale that we could pull off. With Your permission, allow us to put the construct together for proposal? There would be a catch, though, my Goddess."

"And what would that be, baby girl?"

"None of the Dominant men, even the ones on Council, would be allowed to enter the grounds for the entire conference. That would include Daddy, too. NEBU would be run entirely by the Dominas on Council, with the submissive males primarily taking on the manual labor responsibilities of the compound. Of course, since sajira and i are two of the few submissive women who serve Dominas, we would be at Your collective disposal in the manner You see fit."

For the first time in a long time, not one of the Dominas in attendance, including me, could say a word. We were all speechless.

Sin finally broke the silence and conveyed the sentiment for the group. "So, when do we start?"

# TWENTY-FOUR ⊗ SAJIRA

Playing with my sis is always fun, but we were supposed to be working.

Watching Daddy handle things earlier at NEBU was the aphrodisiac we needed to work through these calls and put a little extra sexy on them. I was actually looking forward to tonight, if for nothing else than to take this sexual energy we couldn't unleash on our Dominants and put it to some interesting use.

Work wasn't supposed to be this much fun, but I'd be damned if I was going to say it wasn't getting me horny as hell, either.

The calls were coming hot and heavy most of the night, and the calls that would have normally bored the hell out of me were enhanced by shamise fingering my pussy during the calls, bringing me to the edge so many times I'd lost count. It obviously was working on the customers who were on the listening end of our interludes. My coos and playful moans delighted the age play fetishists who always annoyed me before, and my primal screams delighted the wannabe sadists who fantasized about doing all of these nasty, grimy, depraved, and painful things to me.

If they only knew we knelt to real sadists.

Each call that came in got her going even more, which raised the temperature in the bedroom higher. I racked up the minutes and the time kept flying by. shamise moved between my legs, kissing me during calls and between calls, licking and rubbing my clit, keeping me in a perpetual state of arousal to the point where she was going to get raped if I didn't get relief after I got off work.

Yes, I knew I was supposed to be training her on how to take calls, and I was able to turn the tables for an hour while she fumbled through calls, losing her concentration every time I nibbled on her neck or sucked on her nipples. To watch her squirm and listen to the men get off on her voice was fun and a complete turn-on.

The only downer on the evening was she was still healing from the piercing from a couple of weeks ago, which meant no matter how turned on she was, she couldn't play with her clit until the piercing healed completely.

"Damn, sis, i didn't realize this was so difficult," she said to me during a ten-minute break while we cleaned up a little bit to start another shift. "i didn't think it was that hard. i'm surprised Daddy didn't make us take up exotic dancing."

That thought made me giggle and shiver at the same time. What shamise didn't realize was Ramesses commanded me to bring to him three different options to help with my slut training: exotic dancing and private escorting were the other two options he had to choose for me. In his mercy, he chose the phone sex operator option, thinking it would be the easiest way for the slut training to begin.

Notice that I said *begin*.

But he left the door open to possibly make us into private escorts after the phone sex operator option began to wear thin.

I suspected he was beginning to notice the job was wearing thin on me. Neferterri would have us work at *Liquid* to continue our training if we gave any indication the phone sex thing was beginning to get boring. But they also gave us a six-week window where things would change up, whether we wanted them to or not.

I was nearing the end of the six-week period.

Having shamise starting, at least in my mind, gave me a few more weeks to worry about the next level in my slut training. But I knew the next level was coming, and there wasn't a damn thing I could do to stop it.

Not that I wanted to, mind you. In fact, I was starting to look forward to it in ways I hadn't quite put into real words just yet.

"So, when do we get to hear from your 'Dominant'?" shamise teased, referring to the one call I had yet to get tonight. "i was kinda looking forward to seeing what this dude is about."

"It's touch and go sometimes with him," I had to explain to her. "i usually hear from him, but sometimes he tries to keep me off balance. At first, it was cute, just another fan. But now, it's bordering on the edge of both repulsion and sheer attraction."

I wanted him to call tonight. I think I felt emboldened because shamise was there with me this time around.

The last time he called me, he finally gave me his name, or what I thought was his name. Deion.

I guess that was my first mistake; I could put a name to the person who stirred things up in me.

I did it because he was being so mysterious the whole time, and I caught myself trying to take control of the situation, so I could feel in control.

That went over really well.

All I really accomplished was opening the door to more curiosity about him: what he looked like, whether he was really some loser like I assumed the others were. Deion had a swagger, something similar to Ramesses, which was part of the reason why he was beginning to get under my skin.

Ramesses and I started out when we met at a swinger party a

few years ago. He rubbed me the wrong way at first, too, until a guy got too pushy and Ramesses jacked him up about a foot off the ground. That act really changed my impression of him, and the rest was history.

Deion was having the same effect on me, and I was beginning to feel guilty about it. I mean, I have what I wanted in Ramesses and Neferterri, and even though I'm not entirely thrilled with Ice right now, he satisfied the things I don't get with them.

Still…Deion's getting to me, and I wanted to find out how this would end.

"Well, i am definitely curious to see what happens when he does call. Hell, you can put him on speaker so we both can talk to him," shamise giggled, shifting me out of my thoughts. "He's got your attention, that's for sure, and Daddy's gonna want to know about it."

She was right. They would want to know.

The question was, did I want them to know?

The phone rang, interrupting our conversation. I shook out of my uneasiness and got into character.

"This is Tina, your sex goddess. Can I verify that you are over eighteen, please, before we continue this phone call?" I went into the normal spiel. shamise played with my clit the entire time. I had the phone on speaker the whole night, so the callers could hear every sound.

"Good evening, my Calypso. Must we really go into the unnecessary pleasantries?" my "Sir" came on over the speaker. "I see you've decided to do the speaker phone tonight, good girl. That means I can make you do a few things without your hands on the receiver being an issue."

"Hello, Sir, and yes, i had been waiting for you tonight." I teased him, knowing that I was playing in dangerous territory. "i have my sister slave in the room with me tonight, and she's been dying to find out about you."

"Mmmm, two for the price of one tonight." Deion smirked, and his voice dripped with smugness. "I wonder if I should make you both my bitches tonight."

"Yeah, that will work," shamise whispered in my ear. "He's got a nice voice, but he's not Daddy."

"So, what have you two girls been doing to these poor, unsuspecting saps that needed to get off tonight?" Deion kept it up, his voice suddenly overpowering the vibe in the room. "Have you both been good girls?"

"Yes, Sir," we both cooed at the same time. shamise had already worked a few calls with me, so it was easy for her to chime in when she found the need to.

"So, what do you want us to do, Sir? we've been getting each other off all night, and my pussy's on fire," shamise told Deion, thinking that this was going to be routine.

What she didn't realize was, Deion was not a routine caller.

"Look, slut, I'm not like the other jack-offs that feel the need to feed your ego," Deion sharply snapped, which took shamise off balance. "When you're on the phone, you're on my time and my terms; are we understood?"

*Click.*

"What the fuck did you do that for?" I snapped at shamise without thinking. "I usually get money off this fool."

"sajira, he'll call back." shamise kissed my lips. "They always call back."

About a minute later, Deion was back on.

"Such a feisty bitch, I think it will be interesting and exciting to have you as my prize." Deion didn't seem the least bit upset about having to call back. In fact, I was convinced he was going to rip shamise a new asshole.

That got shamise's attention.

"Your prize, Sir? we belong to someone, so you might have to go through them first," shamise continued, her body slipping between my legs so she could feel the heat rising off my skin. I tried to resist, but I got lost in her scent, too, and we nearly forgot Deion was on the phone when…

"Oh, I don't think Ramesses and Neferterri will mind too much if I borrowed you two for an evening or two."

*Click.*

The line went dead yet again.

# TWENTY-FIVE ∞ SHAMISE

Deion had us shook.

Just when I thought it was safe to be a wanton slut again, and we go and get mixed up with a potential stalker.

sajira and I decided it was best to put it out of our minds after that night. After all, all the security precautions had been accounted for, thanks to Daddy and Dominic, so there was no way for this Deion character to get to us.

Still, the fact he even knew whom we belonged to was enough to stop us dead in our tracks.

sajira panicked and wanted to quit the operator position that night, but I told her we didn't need to alarm Ramesses or Neferterri until we knew there was a credible threat. Knowing her, in her insistence to try and get into his head, she might have compromised herself and told him information that she shouldn't have.

If I learned anything being around my Daddy and my Goddess, especially after the mess I heard about last year with Jasmine kidnapping Daddy, was you can never be too careful.

I made damn sure that was the case.

But that was not what was on my mind tonight.

Tonight was special.

Tonight, I accepted my collar and my place back inside the House of Kemet-Ka.

I was finally home again, permanently, if I had anything to say about it.

I was getting ready to head to the House with sajira. With a few special attendees in the inner circle in attendance, I would graciously and humbly listen for the "click" to make me whole again.

These last six months felt like an eternity, and for a little while, I felt like I would have had to wait for another six months to reclaim what I was willing to foolishly let go.

That was a mistake I wasn't going to make ever again.

"Are you almost ready? Daddy said the car will be by to pick us up in about ten minutes." sajira peeked through the door to check up on me.

"Yes, i'm ready, sis," I replied as I slipped on my heels. "It feels so surreal, almost like déjà vu. It feels like it did four years ago when i was first collared and claimed, and i still have those same butterflies."

"Well, i'm just glad i get to call you family officially after tonight," sajira told me, hugging my neck while I clasped my earrings. "The last collaring ceremony i attended was cool, but this one feels more special because i am personally a part of it."

Yeah, this was special, all right.

And I couldn't wait.

☥

Finally, we were home.

As we got out of the car, I was nervous…very nervous.

But the minute the door opened and both sajira and I were commanded to kneel, strip from the clothes we wore, and crawl to our respective spaces, the nerves immediately disappeared.

Crawling through the front door and into the foyer, it felt as natural to me as walking. The feel of the new home my Daddy and Goddess had built was one of the same closeness and intimacy the old one possessed, despite the fact it was twice the size and on a bigger tract of land.

The marble floor was cold to the touch while on my hands and knees, but I knew better than to complain. Everything was a process with Ramesses and Neferterri, and crawling to our Dominants was one to remind us of our place.

Having my sis there with me was icing on the cake.

The feel of the marble against my skin was soon replaced by the lushness of the carpet leading into the family room. I crawled to my place at the left side of the love seat in the room, while sajira took her place on the right side.

We each assumed the kneeling positions with our arms crossed over our chests, thighs spread, backs straightened, and heads lowered until we were recognized.

I couldn't see anything as my eyes were cast to the floor, but I could feel my Goddess's presence over me, which caused a smile to spread across my lips. Having her energy around me kept me calm, despite the excitement building inside of me.

"Relax, shamise; I can feel your energy starting to rise," my Goddess spoke to me, caressing my cheek. "This is a long time coming, and to make you wait any longer would be torture."

"Yes, m'Lady, i'm trying," I softly answered.

"Good girl. We will start shortly; you know how your Daddy likes to pause for effect," Neferterri told me. I giggled at the thought. Ramesses liked to add suspense. "We also have a few guests to witness the event also."

It didn't matter to me.

My world was about to go back to "normal" in a few hours.

As I kept my position, I heard the other guests entering the house. I didn't dare look up to see whom the voices belonged to, but it wasn't long before the voices edged closer, and began remarking about sajira and me.

"Well, look at these two lovely girls," I heard Mistress Sinsual chime in. "I am so happy to see that she's back."

"Yes, we are quite pleased that she is back where she belongs," I heard Ramesses reply, bringing an even bigger smile to my face.

"she and sajira look absolutely wonderful. You should be proud of both," Master Amenhotep spoke. His voice was one I'd come to love over the years. "But of course, I'm biased because they are a part of My family."

In all, I heard four Dominants in the room and their respective property in attendance for this event. I figured I would be able to speak with the girls, and bois, later on, as they're always giddy to see one of their own have the collar placed around their neck.

I sensed Neferterri move to the center of the room.

"Come to Me, shamise," I heard her command and crawled to her feet, kissing each boot before reassuming my position.

"As You've commanded, my Goddess," I responded, feeling the room temperature rise about ten degrees as I anticipated what was coming next.

I heard the command, "hair," come from behind me from Ramesses.

"As You command, m'Lord," I stated as I pulled my hair up to expose my neck.

After a few seconds, I heard Neferterri whisper in my ear, "It's time, pet. Say the words to complete the circle."

The second she spoke, my mind went completely blank.

After rehearsing it in my head for the weeks leading to this very moment, I couldn't get the words to come out of my mouth.

Inside, I panicked, but I didn't dare show it to anyone in the room. I quickly traveled into my mind to find the words I needed to say to accept the collar and become a part of the family once again.

Finally, after what seemed like an eternity for me—but sajira would tell me later only lasted a few seconds—I finally held my head up, arched my back, and began to utter what needed to be said.

"i am shamise, property of the House of Kemet-Ka. i willfully surrender my mind, body and heart to You, Lord Ramesses and Lady Neferterri. i am Yours to command, without question, without hesitation."

I heard applause once I finished, and I felt two pairs of hands place the collar around my neck. I felt the coolness of the steel and the pendant lay so delicately across my chest.

"Welcome home, precious," I heard from both sides of me, sounding like soothing music to my ears.

Finally, the sweetest sound I'd been waiting for had made its presence known.

*Click*.

☥

Our first House meeting after my collaring was all business.

Damian was in attendance for this portion of the meeting, as Ramesses and Neferterri needed to explain the professional aspects of our service within the House.

I finally got to see what all the fuss was about concerning my potential "brother."

Incest never looked so damn good before. I couldn't stop drooling, at least on the inside.

Hopefully, he had a little "act right" in him, because if he did, my Goddess would surely have a lot of fun breaking him into a proper slave for her service.

Seeing him grab something for Daddy was an unexpected pleasant surprise, though.

For years, as quiet as it had been kept, Neferterri had been trying to acquire a male submissive, but the unfortunate part was finding one who wasn't all about him.

That's not to say female submissives were much better, mind you.

The deal breaker had always been that they only wanted to serve her, thinking they could get away with not being of service to him.

That doesn't work in *this* House.

I shook my head at this fine specimen of a man who moved with a purpose to make sure my Daddy and Goddess were taken care of as they prepared the information we were to receive.

I secretly wondered if Neferterri would allow sajira and me to "welcome" him into the House *properly.*

Properly, meaning fucking the hell out of him.

Damn, did I think that out loud?

Well, hello, he was *fine.*

I'm talking The Rock mixed in with a little Jason Momoa, and tossing in some Boris Kodjoe.

Yeah, *that* kinda fine.

He could potentially have been a lot of fun, but only time would tell.

Once Damian knelt in his position, Ramesses got our attention, and then Neferterri began the meeting.

"Now that the family is here in total, I wanted to explain to you what Ramesses and I have planned regarding your professional capacities with the businesses that we have going right now," she began.

I took to my secondary position, sweeping my legs from under my butt, taking a pen and pad to take the minutes of the meeting. I had a feeling this one was going to be a bit detailed. I was glad I did get comfortable, because they had a lot to say.

"First, Ramesses and I want you three to know we have been very pleased with your growth so far. The next aspect of your servitude is of a professional capacity now," Neferterri started her explanation. "shamise, you will reassume your position as our executive assistant, taking care of any House correspondence, administrative paper-work, and the like. your responsibilities will increase because of the addition of NEBU, *Liquid* and the other businesses we have begun while you were away: the security firm, the mail center, the day-care center and the photography studio has been expanded."

"Yes, Goddess, i understand," I answered. I was excited to have so much to do: six different businesses to handle, and no time clocks to punch or financial worries to consider.

"Which brings us to you, sajira," Neferterri continued, looking in her direction. "you will assume the position of accounting direc-tor, as you will handle the books and oversee all of the accounting departments. I will be relying on you to keep things tight, baby girl. you will be dealing with multimillion-dollar transactions now."

"Yes, Goddess, i understand," sajira responded.

"Lastly, although you have yet to be acquired, Damian, We are going to utilize your health care expertise," Neferterri told him. "It will be of greatest service at NEBU and the other ranch loca-tions, especially with the blood play and medical play enthusiasts that attend events."

"Yes, Ma'am, as You wish," Damian complied.

The sound of his voice made me take even further notice.

Let me stop; I shouldn't be lusting after potential family members, unless Ramesses and Neferterri say it's okay.

You know what they say…the family that plays together, stays together.

"Okay, we have some things to attend to now." Ramesses adjourned the meeting. "We can work out the details over the next few weeks. For now, we have guests to prepare for."

# TWENTY-SIX & RAMESSES

I must say, I'm a bad motherfucker.

Yeah, I know I'm bragging, but if you could see what I saw, you would pat me on the back, too.

I had all of the buildings on the property set in Crimson and Gold, Kemet-Ka colors, completely ablaze, illuminating the night sky.

Inside of each building, potential guests would find a fully stocked kitchen and bar, complete with champagne and wine, to celebrate tonight's festivities. In the common area, a 60-inch HDTV was positioned on the wall over the fireplace in front of the large sectional for entertaining other guests they met and encountered while on the grounds.

In the bedroom, California king-size beds, large enough for couples and their "toys" for the night, spanned the width of the room, giving a bit more space to allow for slaves to sleep on the side of the bed.

Hey, not all Masters and Dominants have their slaves sleep in bed with them, and not all slaves want to sleep in bed with their Masters, either.

I made sure the whirlpool tubs were affixed in each building, and the showers were large enough to support a bench.

One of the doors led to the outside of the bedroom, where an outdoor deck was constructed with the exhibitionists in mind. You know, for the ones that like to show off and scream to attract attention to themselves? Yeah, I had to go there because I loved putting on a show as much as the next one.

Needless to say, I spared no expense to make sure folks kept coming back and telling their friends and associates they needed to be members, too, because, as they say, membership has its privileges.

I wanted to make sure NEBU, and all of the other ranches we had conceived and implemented, were meant for folks to enjoy the comforts, among other things, of the ranches. This was taking the bed and breakfast concept to a whole other level, as far as I was concerned.

I valued as much privacy as could be had, and this was the perfect way to have a lot of other folks be able to do the same thing… for a private membership fee, of course.

I'm sure you could tell there's a running theme here, right? Well, there's a reason for all that, but rather than bore you with the details, just know the legal team we'd put together made sure as many bases had been covered as humanly possible.

I did all the last-minute checking with Dom and the security staff for later on, including the last-minute fail-safes for the extra-curricular activities after the ceremonies were over. With all the alcohol flowing on the premises, someone was liable to get a little wilder than usual, and that needed to be handled in-house.

No police influences.

No exceptions.

After the security sweep, I went back to the main building to check with the service slaves who had volunteered for tonight in the kitchen, the valets and greeters, and the girls who would be taking care of the guests as they mingled and socialized before the formal festivities began.

It would be a grand night indeed.

There was no way in hell I was going to let this night come off without a hitch.

I checked the W Hotel near the airport where the out-of-town guests were staying to touch bases with them and let them know the SUVs would be picking them up as scheduled.

I double-checked with the limo drivers to make sure the rotation schedule at the hotel was on time and clicking. I made a final check with my personal driver to make sure Neferterri, the girls and I would be picked up from home to get back to NEBU before the majority of the guests arrived, so we could receive everyone properly.

Neferterri checked up on the caterers who would be importing the special vegetarian dishes and some international cuisines that were requested by some of the guests, while shamise and sajira kept activity on the online boards in case anyone wanted to be fashionably late and needed last-minute information. sajira also took any payments for people who were serious about attending for tonight, and kept the records clean and organized, while shamise printed the records to keep a paper trail.

Damian kept things fluid with the emergency personnel, letting them know what they needed to be aware of and the things they needed to be prepared for in case someone was in distress. He also coordinated with the dungeon monitors; even though they wanted to state they "knew" what to look for, they were not in the clubs or at the conventions.

I think I've said I was a control freak before, right?

Well, in case you hadn't figured it out by now, I'm a control freak, and I'm more than comfortable with the assessment, thank you very much.

The way I saw it, if I'm willing to pay you for your time, then you need to roll with the rules of the establishment, no matter how new the establishment was.

I was in the midst of finishing up my checklist, when I got a pop-up IM that got my immediate attention:

**sinister_one:** *you do realize that your girls won't be safe tonight, right?*

**lord_ramesses:** *let Me guess, this is the one that's supposed to be able to "take" My girls and show them a good time, right?*

**sinister_one:** *you know, for someone that claims to be the all-knowing Ramesses, you really don't know what's about to happen to the women in your own House*

**lord_ramesses:** *wow, you must be a rookie or something... don't you know it's better to brag AFTER you've pulled off the crime?*

**sinister_one:** *naw, I'd rather tell you first, and then watch the look on your face after it happens*

Yeah, okay.

He could try if he wanted to.

NEBU was locked down pretty tight; Dom and I made sure of it.

I was confused over where this jackass was coming from. I was a bit perturbed because for some reason, I had to get the unstable motherfuckers who thought they could rattle me before every event. Considering the importance of the night's events, I was not in the mood to dismiss ol' boy as an idle threat. So, I made a quick phone call to set some things in motion.

This dude needed to be put on ice quickly, and technology is a beautiful thing.

**lord_ramesses:** *I'll tell you what, you can try, and I'll bury you, literally. Know who you're fucking with first*

**sinister_one:** *see, that's the problem with you wannabe control freaks...*

*you're gonna learn what real control is all about... I'll even bring in one of my boys to help with a tag team rape, just for good measure.*

I considered the possibility that shamise and sajira explained about some dude who'd been playing on the phones while they were doing the phone sex operator thing. I didn't have time to make the wrong decision.

However, I was not one to be insulted by some two-bit wannabe criminal.

I had bigger things to deal with, but I had to show this dude I was not one to be fucked with.

**lord_ramesses:** *well, we'll see how much control you really have... that junk IP address you tried to hit Me up from has already given Me all the information that I need on you... Dunwoody's finest should be at your door in the next few moments*

**sinister_one:** *uh... well... you still can't stop what's gonna happen tonight, even if you did find out where I was, bitch...you better...*

I thought he was going to say something else, but all I saw on the screen was silence.

Wow, I was honestly disappointed.

I wasn't done with the banter.

The next thing I heard was my cell phone.

After seeing the number on my caller ID, it made sense why the "sinister one" was no longer speaking to me by IM.

"We got him, Kane," Officer Candon, whose submissive happened to be helping out at NEBU tonight, told me over the phone. "He won't be bothering You too much tonight."

"Thanks, Officer Candon," I replied, keeping it professional between us so there would be nothing to trace back in court. "I hope You have enough information, and if not, I can come in and make a statement in the morning."

"Not a problem, Sir," Candon followed my lead, keeping up the pretenses for dude to hear. "Terroristic threats don't require a lot when it's all in cyberspace. He tried to purge his system, but his IP can be traced. This dude's not too smart."

Yeah, that's an understatement.

So, after dealing with that bit of stupidity, I kept on with the checklist, shaking off the expected chills that came with a close call.

The next step was to get dressed and prepare for tonight.

It's time to show off the new place.

# TWENTY-SEVEN ⚭ SAJIRA

My time to shine…

Leaving from my soon-to-be permanent owners' home with anticipation of what lay ahead, my excitement for this party, my formal collaring being the centerpiece of the party, I knew my life would change the moment I heard the collar lock around my neck. Arriving to NEBU, I looked at all of the subsequent cottages leading to the main house. The lighting of the house took my breath away. There were lights everywhere.

I sat in the Navigator limousine we rode in and watched with amazement as the sub bois checked the cars in, checking invitations and letting those in who had the required documentation to be there. I drooled over some of the outfits I saw, taking mental inventory over the divas I would ask where they bought their outfits from, so I could find a way to rock the outfits at the next event.

Wait, let me change that last phrase…so I could find a way to rock *better* outfits at the next event.

See, the atmosphere at NEBU was, well, I could only describe as basically something out of a fashion magazine, the fashionistas of the BDSM world, just like in N.Y. during fashion week and the "who's who" came out to see and be seen. It wasn't hard to figure out I had become a part of the BDSM Elite, among the other people who were being closely screened and scrutinized.

I was amazed at all the fuss that was being made over my collaring ceremony: subs stood at the front of the house beside the driveway, adorned in leather. There were other submissives lining the main walkway throwing rose petals, giving us a royal entrance, so to speak. I could tell that Ramesses and Neferterri had made sure every detail was set to give the night a more Afrocentric feel. I was somewhat embarrassed by all the attention, but beaming with pride as I walked in with them. Along the walls leading to the dungeon area, male subs with erect shafts held hard by cock rings were standing at attention while female subs bowed as we walked by.

"Are you okay, sajira?" I heard Neferterri ask of me, no doubt sensing my nervousness as we walked by all of the guests. Ramesses walked ahead of us, shaking hands with those who were already mingling before we arrived. "I can imagine this is a lot to take in."

Considering Ice and I didn't get a chance to see the "Red Carpet" festivities before safi's collaring ceremony last year, it would have been different if I had seen the spectacle before going through my own. I would have been better prepared for what was going on in my honor.

"Yes, my Goddess, i'm trying to adjust to all this. i'm really nervous," I sheepishly answered, lowering my eyes in respect as I was trained to do. I felt her hand caress my cheek before she kissed my lips, as if to silently reassure me things were okay.

Each room in the Main House was attended to by a male or female slave, completely naked, constantly at the beck and call. They had been given orders to do what was asked of them, within reason, Ramesses told me. "NO water sports or scat play of any kind, as an example of an extreme request." I remembered. I saw one male sub standing with his shaft erect and with his hands tied above his head. His main duty was to stand there without letting it go limp. Dominas, the ones who were into CBT, or cock and ball torture, would slap it, beat it. Even his Mistress would torment him, but he would not move.

I was allowed permission to roam around for a while, as the main event, my ceremony, would not begin for a good half hour, so I took that moment to do a little exploring within the House, to assuage my curiosity. One of the rooms I came to was different than all the rest, it was dark and cold, but yet inviting me in to indulge. It was like going into the unknown. I entered the room and the sub who attended the room bowed his head and said, "Please enter, Madam."

I blushed at the thought. He assumed I was a Domina, but I entered the room anyway. I saw slaves chained to the wall, being tormented, although not painfully, but being teased to the point of orgasm and then having to stop. There were other male subs on their knees pleasing the Dominas in the room, female submissives being flogged or paddled, and some who were being chained to the wall as a live piece of art.

I was a nervous wreck. I was hot, I was sweating, and I wanted to be on my knees at that moment. I wanted to feel what they felt, but I knew in time that would come. I left that room to explore others, seeing all the different rooms and toys. I couldn't understand why I tortured myself; all of the visual stimulation made me all the more excited. I needed to leave before I found myself in the midst of a frenzy I couldn't recover from.

I walked outside to the garden where submissives were being used as decorations, seeing Masters and Mistresses trading their submissives for services. Female submissives crawled on the ground, being led as property and chattel, while the male submissives endured being beaten or being taken by their Dominas with strap-on dildos.

This was all new to me. I never got to see a lot of the time. It was exciting as hell to witness and take in. When I felt I could go back inside, I walked into yet another room, where I witnessed a male sub ordered to sit on this glass phallus, and a huge one, I might add, and he was forced to suck every dick placed in his mouth. He enjoyed himself way too much, which got his ass beat, but I think he did that shit on purpose.

One of the NEBU submissives came up to me and placed her hand on my shoulder softly. "sajira, your Lord and Lady request your presence in the dungeon," she stated. She then took my hand and led me to the dungeon.

We got down to the dungeon, and I could tell it would be an extraordinary night. Mistress Sinsual was there, along with my husband and tiger, Mistress Blaze and her Leather family was in attendance, as was Master Altar and his girl, chastity. I recognized a few others from the last time I was here, before my awakening.

My senses were overwhelmed with the smells of lavender, amber and rose. The scents caused my body to betray me, tingling with desire. The extra fragrance of fresh jasmine in the air brought my emotions to the boiling point. Looking around the dungeon, I noticed the nakedness of the submissives, their poise, their posture, their reverence to the Dominants and Masters in the room. I noticed male subs sitting at the feet of their Mistresses, including my husband, kissing the feet of the passersby. I scanned the room, noticing the female submissives kneeling at the feet of their Masters, kissing the midsections of the other Dominants walking by, bowing in reverence if no kiss was required. It was an amazing sight to behold.

Seeing my husband at the feet of his Domina, I really didn't know what to think. I'd been training my mind to separate the husband I knew and loved from the submissive male I walked past as he abided by the commands of Mistress Sin. That, in and of itself, had been a process that hadn't been the easiest for me, but I loved him deeply.

I was taken into a preparation room where Neferterri supervised as I was stripped naked and adorned with the most elaborate pieces of satin. My hair was braided into one long ponytail with ribbons and flowers, those of which she had chosen: white baby's breath and miniature pink roses. My body was oiled to make it shimmer and shine in the light.

I never felt so sexy, so sensual, in my life.

The slave girls took my training collar and attached the chains that led from them and clipped onto my nipples. My wrists and ankles had leather straps around them with silver attachment hooks, I thought. I stood before my Goddess with my hair braided, neutral-colored makeup applied, adorned in leather and diamonds looking as though I were a submissive goddess.

Neferterri hugged me and said, "you are not allowed to speak once you enter the chambers. Remember the words you are to speak once your ceremonial scene is over with Master Altar, little one. I know you will be floating, but you must be mindful of your surroundings. Do you understand Me?"

"Yes, my Goddess, i understand. i hope to make You proud of me." There was a trembling in my voice, and I had hoped to see Ramesses before the ceremony began. If for nothing else, I needed his voice in my ear to calm me.

Being led to my kneeling bench for the pleasure of the Masters in attendance, I really didn't know where to focus or whom to focus on. The room was dim with candle lights, with beautiful Dominas and Masters sitting all about. The submissives walked around serving drinks, food, or simply saying, "i am at your service."

I was scared, nervous, but excited because in my mind, I knew this was who I was. Being placed in the center of the room, I stood with my hands above my head, legs spread wide apart, for the audience to look at me, to gaze at me, to fondle me. I maintained my position, but my insides were on fire, and my skin felt white-hot to the touch.

Tonight was the night my Lord and Lady were giving to me, my moment to shine. I wished I could see the submissives around me, but I imagined some of them beaming, and others trying not to show how jealous they were that they were not on display as I was at that moment. I would have never done this in a swingers' environment, but for some reason, Ramesses and Neferterri both have helped me find my freedom within the constraints of my collar, the leather wrist and ankle cuffs that I wore. I felt like the sexiest bitch alive.

Master Altar then publicly asked, "With Your permission, Lord Ramesses and Lady Neferterri, I would like to begin the ceremonial scene."

"You may begin, Master Altar," Neferterri answered.

After placing me on the Cross to begin the scene, Master Altar removed the collar and nipple clamps and placed a different pair of nipple clamps on, starting with my left nipple. I wanted to scream, but it didn't stop him. He said, "I understand, but pain can lead to exquisite pleasure." He placed the other clamp on the right nipple, but by then, I was moaning. "Shhh… be mindful of your surroundings, little one. your owners are watching."

I never knew pain could be so exciting, but I wanted more. Master Altar pulled on the clamps, sending my body into this reaction that it needed more. He began quietly telling me how beautiful and how soft and satiny my skin was, telling me I should be proud to be owned by such honorable Dominants.

He whispered, "I want you to relax. I am about to start the ceremonial scene now." He started with light strokes with the flogger, and again I was moaning, but I knew I should be quiet so I bit my lip. He was going faster and harder and I silently begged that I wanted more.

Swish…

Swoosh…

In the air I heard the flogger come down. I anticipated the sting, but what I kept feeling was more pleasure, and a guilty pleasure at that. My ass was stinging, and I was supposed to be in pain, but he never stopped. Master Altar then took out the pinwheel and ran it across my thighs and back. I was startled, but he didn't stop.

Master Altar began grabbing my hair, pulling me back, and I screamed in my mind, *I want it, damn it…don't stop.* He paddled my already throbbing ass, and I couldn't recall how hard. I was soaring, but my body moved and swayed, telling him I wanted more. I waited for the pause as he took a break to grab the next thing to use on me during the scene.

I enjoyed being on the Cross and feeling the stinging effects of the leather flogger, the paddle, whatever he chose that was at his disposal, but I never used my safeword. I was so excited my body shivered and shook from the inside out. I was not afraid; he was not going to hurt me, not with my owners present.

He stood behind me, massaging my body, showcasing the marks he so carefully placed on my ass. I was so mentally exhausted, but I was nearly complete. I was hoping to be able to move my body once the restraints were unshackled from the Cross, but my arms and legs felt heavy.

Master Altar enlisted the help of another Dominant, although I really don't remember whom it was. All I remembered was another pair of hands helping me down off the Cross, and slowly bringing me back to the kneeling bench. It was at that time when Neferterri's voice rang in my head to remember the pledge to complete the ceremony.

"With devotion, i offer my body, my mind, and will to You, m'Lord and m'Lady, to care for and do with as You will. Your desires are mine, Your will is my command." I recited proudly, taking every effort to utter those words because my body was recovering from the effects of the scene.

The next thing I felt was my hair being lifted from my shoulders and the collar being clasped around my neck. I then heard Ramesses' voice proclaim to the audience, "I now present to you our sajira, submissive princess of the House of Kemet-Ka." The roar of the applause from the crowd was exhilarating. I felt a blanket fall around my shoulders and felt them both walk me toward a couch nearby to bring me out of my space intact.

"We are very proud of you, sajira," I heard my Goddess say to me. I leaned against her shoulder, taking sips of ice water and eating some cookies, which was what I remembered telling them I would want to help bring me out of subspace. "How do you feel, little one?"

The warmth I felt from the collar around my neck, the blanket warming my body back to some sense of normalcy, and feeling the energy from being between my owners was indescribable. I felt Ramesses kissing my forehead, which helped complete my travel out of subspace. "I feel absolutely euphoric right now. Thank You for accepting me into Your world. I love You both so much."

# TWENTY-EIGHT ☮ RAMESSES

"Folks, I have an important announcement of My own to make." I heard Amenhotep proclaim after everyone finished congratulating us on sajira's collaring. I wasn't sure what I heard, but the seriousness in His tone had my undivided attention, whether I wanted it to or not. "I believe this is long overdue, and My fellow gentlemen and ladies would agree with this."

I turned my head in His direction, trying to figure out what the hell my Mentor was talking about. I sat with sajira, stroking her hair and enjoying the moment, basking in the glow she emanated from being on full display. Neferterri, seated on the other throne, and shamise, happily nestled between Neferterri's legs, acted like they were completely in the dark and had no clue of what was going on. Damian, who knelt on the outside of Neferterri's chair, only smiled as he listened closely to Amenhotep's speech.

If I knew anything about my girls, they were horrible actresses when they wanted to keep something from me. Damian and I had yet to get to that level, so he was no help in trying to figure out what was about to happen. One look from me and they melted in moments, dying to spill the beans. When I noticed they weren't acting, I was at a total loss as to what was up His sleeve.

The problem now came in the form of an enigmatic question: what in the world was inside the mind of Master Amenhotep? When

He wanted to play something close to the vest, there was a snowball's chance in hell of anyone getting the information out of Him.

I looked at Osiris and saw nothing.

Seti wasn't much help, and neither was Menes.

I scanned around for anyone to give me an idea, and my frustration rose with each passing second.

The crowd fell silent as Amenhotep stepped between the twin thrones to speak from a better vantage point.

I'm sure the befuddled look on my face was one for the history books, but it was genuinely warranted. The last time Amenhotep sprang a surprise on me was when I "inherited" the Palace and a small fortune. Only the gods knew what the hell He could be announcing.

"As most of you know, Ramesses and I began our journey together nearly fifteen years ago when He was just a young man…not that He's still not a young man, but you all know what I mean."

That comment drew laughter in the room.

After the laughter died down, He continued. "I have watched Him grow up, keeping a calming influence when it was needed, and letting Him make mistakes along the way, even if I didn't want Him to."

I felt sajira squeeze my hand. She felt the emotions stirring within me. I was happy she could feel me while we were in this moment, and I knew Neferterri and shamise could feel me also. A lot of what He said triggered nostalgic thoughts from deep within that I always selfishly drew upon whenever I got into a position where I needed to focus. Those thoughts were being brought to the forefront with each word Amenhotep spoke.

"I have selfishly wished and prayed for the day where a man I thought of as a son, and in some instances, I did 'raise' Him within

this realm, would join Me within the ranks of the inner circle…
the *Neb'net Maa'kheru.*" He looked down at me, and in an instant
I was twenty years old again, completely new, raw, and transparent
to the audience that hung on His every word, wondering what
He could be speaking of.

Neferterri heard the reference to the Society, and her facial expression almost gave her away. By then I was too far gone to notice.
I was trapped in the lessons, the intense discussions we'd had at
the beginning of my mentoring with Him. I chuckled at the questions I asked back then, the constant battling because I thought I
knew better, and the patience He was able to exert despite my
sheer ignorance of things.

"Tonight, with the blessings of the other members, I welcome
You, Ramesses, within the *Neb'net Maa'kheru.*" Amenhotep extended
His hand out to me, gripping it as I rose from my throne to em-
brace him.

The applause would have been deafening if I'd paid attention
to it, but all I heard were the words, "I love You, son," coming from
my "father." Seti, Osiris, Menes, and the other men flooded the
throne area, offering their congratulations and well-wishes, laughing at the lack of words coming from my mouth.

Hell, why wouldn't I be speechless? I looked around at men whose
walks were years ahead of my own. For them to include me at this
point in my journey was beyond my ability to articulate.

Master Osiris moved to the front of the group, his smile beaming
as he looked at me. I was still struggling to find words to express
my euphoria while in this moment. He held a case in his hand,
sending my mind into a new level of confusion, trying to figure
out what the case was for.

"Ramesses, we within the *Neb'net Maa'kheru* would like to present You with this ring, which is recognized within our respective communities as that of a Master of Honor." Osiris smiled as he held the opened case.

I stood astonished upon viewing the diamond and platinum-encrusted ring, complete with "Ramesses" on one side of the ring, and the word "Master" emblazoned on the other. My eyes moved immediately to my Beloved, who watched with pride as I slipped on the ring, blushing slightly as I cut my eyes at her, knowing she stealthily had revealed my ring size.

"Congratulations, Daddy!" I heard shamise yelling through the applause. I leaned over and kissed her forehead and then her lips, letting her know I heard her clearly.

The next moment, Lady Hatshepsut stepped onstage with Amenhotep. I found my throne and had taken my seat to reclaim sajira, oblivious to her presence. "Master Amenhotep, I would like to make My own announcement, if I may, Sir?" she asked.

"By all means, My dear." Amenhotep stepped to the side. "After You, M'Lady, the floor is Yours."

Now it was time for both Neferterri and I to wonder what the hell was really going on. This was only supposed to be a grand reopening of NEBU, but this was turning into something damn near legendary before it was all said and done.

"Ladies and gentlemen, it gives Me great pleasure to announce the formation of a Society similar to what the esteemed Gentlemen have within *Neb'net Maa'kheru*," Lady Hatshepsut began. "With the generosity of the members of *Neb'net Maa'kheru*, we have established the Ladies of Beauty & Honor, forever to be known as *Nebet'new Nefrew Maa'kheru*."

The surprise on our faces gave the audience more reason to applaud loudly, especially the Dominas in attendance.

Lady Hatshepsut smiled more and waited for the applause to

die down before she continued. "With the creation of the Ladies' Society, the rings have also been fashioned and ready to be presented to the Ladies that will be the charter members of *Nebet'new Nefrew Maa'kheru*."

Neferterri looked down at shamise, who was the only House member who knew such information to be able to give to Lady Hatshepsut to get the sizing correct. shamise immediately blushed, knowing she'd been able to keep things under lock and key until this very moment. Neferterri kissed her forehead and mouthed something I couldn't make out, but I had a feeling a pseudo-punishment was on the horizon.

"So, I present to you all: Mistress Sinsual, Mistress Blaze, Lady Norene, Lady Ethereal, and finally, Lady Neferterri." As Lady Hatshepsut called each of the ladies' names, the NEBU male slaves happily knelt at the feet of each charter member, assuming the kneeling position and presenting the ring cases to them.

The ladies were speechless. The expressions of each of their faces, including my wife's, was priceless. My Beloved looked at me in an accusatory manner, like I had something to do with it, and I held my hands up in an authentic gesture. I really did not know that this was going to be brought to witness.

The grins were genuine and radiant.

The night couldn't have gone any better.

Amenhotep found a way to shatter the statement in a way I never saw coming.

"I want it known, as we speak from this point forward, that Lord Ramesses now be recognized as Master Ramesses." Amenhotep concluded his speech. "As such, His slaves will no longer refer to Him as Lord, but as Master. The community, having publicly voiced their approval, shall recognize Master Ramesses as an honorable Master within this realm."

He then presented me with His Master's cap.

The blank expression on my face told Him I didn't deserve it.

The look of pride on His face told me no one else deserved it more.

"To begin Your legacy, My son, You will need this. I expect this to be in good hands until such time as You will present it to Your protégé one day." Amenhotep finally shed tears, something I'd seen Him do rarely. "This is My final gift to You, to complete the circle."

The crowd applauded once more at seeing the reverence I still didn't believe I deserved just yet. I would never feel I did, but I had to come to the conclusion that, whether I thought I deserved it or not, the community deemed me worthy.

I would have to make peace with it, in my own time.

But for now, there was more partying to do.

"Congratulations, my Master."

I had no intentions of being this naturally high tonight, but obviously other folks had plans for me. I continued to allow the flood of good feelings swirling around the compound to continue.

I was in a circle of conversation with Master Seti, Amenhotep and Master Osiris, discussing the plans we had for the other two compounds. We wanted to make sure we were on the same page for the morning send-offs tomorrow.

Neferterri sat next to me, placing her input where it was needed, while shamise, sajira and Damian were in relaxed positions at the base of our chairs, silently enjoying the flow of information.

I didn't know if I could get used to the title yet.

*Master...this was the next level.*

I promised myself I would weigh the significance of tonight's events, because they were heavy indeed.

The rest of the night was reserved for celebrating.

And celebrate I would, because there was much to celebrate, on a lot of different levels.

Life was blessed right now.

"Master, may shamise and i be excused, please?" I heard sajira ask of me. "i left something inside in the limousine i need for the cooler weather later tonight."

Neferterri objected. "you're not leaving, not without an escort, girls. you both know your Daddy and I don't like it when you're away from either of us without knowing where you're going."

I cut a look at her, winking quickly in her direction before the girls could catch on. "Security is tight on the compound tonight, Beloved, and there haven't been any reports from security tonight of any unauthorized entries. They will be fine."

I saw the nervous looks on our girls' faces. The whole mess with Deion still had them shook, and I couldn't blame them. With security at the soft spots within the compound, and cameras covering every other blind spot in or around NEBU, I had no problems with letting them quickly head to the car and back.

"Okay, you heard your Master; be back in about ten minutes," Neferterri explained to them.

"Yes, my Goddess, we won't be long," sajira replied as they headed out of the room.

"Are You sure about this, Beloved?" Neferterri asked, still a little concerned.

"Yes, baby, I promise, things will work out fine," I reassured her, considering this was her first time going through this. "You'll see. Everything is going according to plan."

# TWENTY-NINE ⊗ SHAMISE

I couldn't figure out where I was.

The blindfold over my eyes let me know my captors had no intention of letting me know where I was or what was going to happen to me.

I felt the lushness of the comforter we helped select for the beds, and the coolness of the air against my skin let me know that we hadn't left the safety of the compound.

But that didn't mean I wasn't out of harm's way, as the binds on my arms and legs made their presence known.

Then another scary thought came to my mind.

Where was sajira?

The last thing I remembered was heading out to the limousine with her to grab something she forgot so we could head back in and enjoy the festivities down in the dungeon Daddy just unveiled. I felt a quick rush of air, then something slammed over my mouth, and I saw a figure grab sajira and try to do the same thing to her.

Then everything went dark.

The grogginess I felt made me wonder if they used some noxious agent to incapacitate us both. The lingering smell on my lips confirmed it: chloroform.

As tight as security was, and had always been, at NEBU, how in the hell could we have possibly been kidnapped and brought into one of the buildings on the compound without tipping anyone off?

My mind raced through the possibilities, wondering if because of the huge crowd that was being handled, and the fact that sajira and I had left the sight of Daddy and Goddess without an escort, someone took advantage of the situation and decided we could be had whether we wanted to be or not.

Someone wanted to prove a point.

In my mind, the point was proven, definitely.

Now the question became whether I was alone or whether sajira was anywhere near me.

My hearing heightened, tuning in to the moans and whimpers of my sis close to me on a separate bed in the room we were in.

It scared me because I couldn't figure out what she was moaning about. Whether it was from fear, or pain, or pleasure, I couldn't tell because my own fear gripped me tightly and wouldn't let go.

At the same time…it made me wet.

Extremely wet.

I felt ashamed my body responded in the way it did, knowing good and well we could both have been in real danger.

I heard the familiar sound of steel scraping against a sheath, and two distinctly different voices talking amongst themselves.

The minute I couldn't recognize either of them as Daddy's, I knew we were in for a long night.

"Who's there, why are you doing this to us?" I shouted out toward the voices. "sajira, are you okay?!?!"

*SLAP!*

"Say something again, bitch, and you will be in for a world of hurt, you understand?!?!" I recognized the voice immediately as Deion.

Fuck. How the hell did he get on the compound???

*"Leave her alone!"* I heard sajira yelling.

*SLAP!*

That sound came from sajira's direction, trying to shut her up.

"We are playing by MY rules now, understand, bitch?" I heard the other guy tell sajira. I couldn't recognize his voice, but it was powerful and deep.

It still didn't belong to Daddy, and Goddess was nowhere in sight or sound, either.

That was not a good sign.

"Yes, we are playing by your rules," I heard sajira reply, but I heard lust in her voice. I imagined the fear was somehow being replaced by the adrenaline to get her through it.

Feeling the sharp blade against my skin, I struggled against the weight of Deion's muscles against my chest.

The next thing I felt was the binds being cut from my ankles, which freed my legs to do what I wanted.

Or what I thought I wanted.

Instead of kicking him in the balls, which might have taken things to the next level, something weird happened.

No matter how badly my instincts told me that I needed to fight for my life.

No matter how much I wanted to find something sharp to gouge his eyes out, despite the blade in his hand, or quite possibly something more dangerous, and help my sis, who I felt was in as much danger as I was in.

I couldn't wait for him to take me.

As repulsive as his scent was to me, and as gruff and disgusting as his beard was against my skin, all I wanted to do was to fight him so he could get angry enough to take me hard and deep and treat me as nothing more than a common whore in the back seat of a piece of shit Pontiac.

Our shared deepest, darkest fantasy was coming true.

And neither of our owners was here to witness.

But then I had a strange thought, which couldn't be helped because my mind was working a mile a minute trying to make sense of it all.

What if they were here, watching the whole thing?

Considering sajira and I were both tightly blindfolded, with no real possibility of seeing any of this unfold, there was no way to know.

But we also never got the chance to tell them this was what we wanted, either.

He put the blade against my neck and spread my legs wide, taking the knife to my top, shredding it to let me know that the blade was sharp enough to cut me deep.

"Now, here's how this is going to go down, bitch," he calmly spoke, with a coldness that let me know we were nothing more than holes to either of them. "you will address both of us as Sir, if we even allow you to speak. you will be used and abused by us until we decide you can't take any more, and then we'll leave you here for your 'Master' to find you in the morning. Do you understand?"

I went into shock, my fight instincts taking over.

I heard sajira yell, "Fuck you! When our Daddy and Goddess find out, they will fuck you up!"

I yelled out with her, "If we don't get to you first! You're so bad with two helpless bitches not being able to fight back!"

My wrists were immediately cut in response to my yelling, and the screams I heard from sajira and the sounds from the series of slaps and punches I heard her taking, let me know they were more than willing to put the term "helpless bitches" to the test.

I felt a different pair of hands grabbing my throat, roughly whispering in my ear, "you're mine now, slut. Look at you, already wet and ready for me to take this pussy."

*"Fuck you!"* I yelled back at him, causing him to close even tighter around my throat. He laughed at my struggling to breathe, rubbing his other hand against my clit.

I was upset at myself for wanting this to happen, but my body had other ideas on what it needed.

"I thought you were supposed to be a wanton slut? You're supposed to be ready to take it anytime and anywhere, right?"

I knew Deion had already begun fucking sajira, because I heard him moan out, "Aww, shit, just as tight as I thought it would be! Damn, you feel so good!"

I heard muffled moaning and screaming from sajira, which had me wondering if a gag had been put over her mouth or if Deion had put his hand over her mouth while he fucked her.

I felt pressure inside of my walls as my captor entered inside of me.

At that point, I froze.

This motherfucker was not about to do this, not without a fight.

The tears flowed freely, but the excitement in my body kept building as I struggled against what my mind did not want to happen and what my body was so willing to allow. I was scared for sajira, as I continued to hear her moans and screams, frantically trying to figure out if she was trying to fight or if her body betrayed her the same way that it had done a number on me.

I was determined to not let my body win.

"Get the fuck off me, now!" I started clawing at him, not thinking to take my blindfold off now that my hands were free. I would have wanted to see the people doing this to us; neither of us asked for this to go down.

Or did we?

The next sounds I heard came from sajira, growling and sounding like she was in an entranced state, yelling at Deion, "Fuck this pussy, motherfucker! You won't get another whiff of this shit, you weak-ass bitch! You better beat it up, you sonofabitch!"

My captor egged him on, "Fuck that bitch, man. Make that pussy yours!"

I fell into my own trance, inhaling my arousal. The primal aroma rising from my essence was evident as he kept the blade at my neck. Whatever fear I had turned to acquiescence to my desires. I clawed his back, making sure I struck blood as he tried to go as deep as he could inside of my pussy.

"Is that all you got, bitch? I thought you wanted to beat this pussy up?!?!" I taunted him, my instincts taking over, worried about my survival and sajira's more than anything else. I was willing to say or do anything to get this over with.

I hated my body wanted this to continue, so I used Daddy to keep my mind into it. If I didn't, I knew my body would stop immediately.

I secretly hoped sajira tried to do the same thing, prayed she hadn't completely given in to Deion. I wanted to fight for her, but I had my own fight to worry about.

"Whatever, bitch, you want this dick; your pussy's wet taking it all in." He grunted, pinning my legs down so he could drive deeper inside me. He wasn't all that large, but he was long, and I could feel him damn near hit the bottom with each stroke.

I heard sajira growling louder by the second, the pitch in her voice signaling her orgasm was on the verge of eruption.

"Take this pussy, Sir; please, I've been a bad slut! Hurt me, please!"

"Yeah, bitch, I knew you'd come around; come on my dick!"

I heard him trying to keep from coming, trying to stay as best as he could inside her. I guess sajira had found his button to get this over with.

I couldn't stop myself from coming with my captor inside of

me, but I wasn't going to give him the satisfaction of thinking that he got me "there."

With the blindfold on, he couldn't see the tears starting to flow from my eyes as the orgasm began to take my body and engulf my senses. The fabric mercifully soaked the tears before they could run down my cheek, and I held my ground to keep from floating into subspace with him still stroking me.

I was not going to let him win, but it felt like a Pyrrhic victory. The guilt of betraying Daddy and Goddess was too much to bear.

I felt him about to come, and he suddenly pulled out of me, the sound of the condom snapping let me know that he was trying to explode in my mouth.

That I couldn't allow.

I couldn't hear sajira anymore, and I couldn't figure out if something happened to her or not, but this jackass was not going to break the rules.

He'd have to kill me first.

I felt his member coming close to my mouth, and before he could finish the job, I took my fist and connected with his balls.

"Oh my God, that bitch just...owww fuckkkk!!!" he shouted, trying to protect himself before I decided to really get rough.

I pulled the blindfold off my face for the first time, trying to focus my eyesight so I could continue to beat him senseless, make him pay for even thinking about doing something he had no business trying. I had a hard time figuring out where everyone was, but I got tackled from behind and restrained while face-down on the bed.

"shamise!!! No!!!"

Those were the only words I heard from sajira before my mouth was covered and I inhaled the fumes once again.

# THIRTY ⚵ NEFERTERRI

I watched Damian intently.

"Strip, slave, and put on what I have for you," I commanded.

The room was cool, which contrasted with the unyielding heat of the outside area we'd left from.

We were sitting in the master bedroom suite, preparing for the slave auction that was to start shortly. This was the fun part of the evening for me; it was one of the rare times I got to enjoy things without Ramesses being around. He was still in heavy conversation with the other men, discussing a myriad of topics, from politics to economics, sports to God knows what else.

I smiled wickedly at the nervousness consuming him. His hands twisted together over and over again like he'd had a moment of a crisis of conscience.

*What the fuck have I just gotten myself into?* I imagined him saying to himself. He had no idea, but he was soon about to find out.

On the floor, at my feet, was a box big enough to hold an outfit I'd especially picked out for tonight's occasion.

As he approached, crawling to me, I resisted the urge to command him to please me orally. There would be time for that later. First, there was something I wanted to know, and I was going to find out tonight.

As he knelt to pick up the box, I said to him, "Shower and dress in the piece in the box, and get ready for the next phase of things to come, pet."

"Yes, Goddess," he responded. "Your command is my will."

I watched as he took the box and headed for the bathroom, envisioning the grin on his face as he disappeared behind the door to shower.

I didn't make it a practice to give gifts to submissives we had not yet acquired. I kinda broke that rule with sajira, but we had known her in a different way long before she became a part of the House. Damian had yet to be given a possibility of a name, and while we had begun the process of incorporating him into the professional side of things, we had yet to place him under any type of consideration.

That would also change tonight.

Having him at my feet with sajira and shamise and watching the scowls on the faces of some of the Dominas and Masters who had yet to have one to call their own, it became clear he was a rare prize indeed, and he needed to be claimed.

After all, he had been compliant and obedient this entire time.

My thoughts were interrupted by Damian coming out in the outfit he would be wearing for the auction tonight.

Oh...my...God! He looked good enough to...

*Okay, Neferterri, calm down.*

I licked my lips and prayed to the gods I didn't rape him right there on the spot.

Seeing his body exposed except for the pair of leather boxer briefs, complete with a slot on the fabric that allowed for a pair of handcuffs to be attached to the waistband, I was worried that my prayers wouldn't be answered before it was time to greet guests.

It wasn't a coincidence I had the cuffs ready to be hooked to him.

"How do You like, Goddess?" Damian slightly blushed as he did a quick turn, allowing me the pleasure of seeing the cloth from the front and the back.

"I love it, Damian." I smirked, knowing some lucky bitch was going to have to come off some serious cash and stave off a bidding war in order to temporarily have what's mine. "Are you ready to head downstairs now?"

"Yes, Goddess, at Your command."

Yeah, I could get used to this.

There would be a half-dozen male submissives and slaves who would be participating in the auction, including tiger and Ice, who also would be going through this for the first time. I wasn't gonna lie, though; I was curious about a few things going on within Damian I needed to make happen. Not to mention the fact that I planned to make a certain submissive male happy at the same time by bidding on him to take care of a fantasy of my own.

And I would make it happen.

Ramesses wasn't the only one who got what he wanted.

♀

"Now this prime piece of property comes from a most gracious Domina."

I giggled at seeing the flushed and embarrassed look on Damian's face as he listened at what was being said about him as he knelt on the auction block. I knew it would make him uncomfortable, but it wasn't about his pleasure. It was my pleasure to see him squirm, and I enjoyed his want to please me despite his discomfort.

That's what I wanted in our slaves.

It made me proud to know he was finally getting it.

It made me horny to realize the limits that could be pushed at my whim.

"He is trained in all forms of worship, especially gifted in oral worship, and has strong endurance, according to his Goddess." Lady Hatshepsut kept going, playing to the ladies in the crowd. "She also states he is a pain slut, and is well versed in various massage techniques and has been given permission by his Goddess to obey the commands of the Domina or Master who wins the bid for him."

There was a raucous applause when the women heard that.

"Now, ladies, I will have one of the NEBU slaves sample Damian's abilities," Lady Hatshepsut stated, to the chagrin of the ladies who wanted to find out for themselves before bidding.

The sighs coming from the NEBU slave was all the audience needed to get its collective lather going, a slow rumble of conversation wafting through the crowd. In all, I would say about a good twenty women were in competition with each other, with the strict stipulation that owners could not bid on their own property, making things even more interesting.

The sigh of approval from her and moans and orgasmic sounds being amplified from the microphone preceded the furious bidding war for Damian. He fervently lapped at her, causing her to grab his head instinctively and grind her hips against his tongue. My pussy twitched, remembering his oral presentation from earlier in the week.

"Do I hear a starting bid of five hundred dollars for this beautiful boi?" Lady Hatshepsut began.

"Five hundred!"

"Do I hear a thousand?"

Okay, look, I didn't say this was for those with budgets, did I?

"Two thousand!" I heard from another Mistress behind me.

I was glad this money was going to charitable causes, and from the way the men were at each other's throats over the female submissives, those charities were going to be happy with us.

By the time they were done with Damian, he was won for $7,500.

Anyone who said men were pigs had never been to a male revue or a male auction.

I was content with allowing the ladies to do what they wanted during the auction. After all, being the Lady of the House did have its benefits, and I would soon have what I wanted in a few hours.

The night was still young.

# THIRTY-ONE ⊗ NEFERTERRI

"Now, tell Me how much you want to suck his dick, pet," I told Damian.

I felt his uneasiness as he assessed the pure bluntness of my statement. He was unsure of himself, visibly shaking, trying to measure his words to me in response.

I didn't resist the pleasure I got from watching his wheels turn in his head. If anything, it enhanced my arousal, giving me an endorphin rush I would ride the rest of the night.

"Please, Goddess, may i? i really want to," he begged.

I smiled, but I wasn't satisfied with the answer.

"I don't know, you don't sound sincere enough for Me," I teased, but with a hint of seriousness in my voice. "you haven't properly answered My question. Ask again."

"Please, my Goddess, may i please? i really, really want to…"

Damian kept hesitating, so I folded my arms and sternly commanded, "I don't think you heard Me, bitch; do you want to suck tiger's dick?"

Damian swallowed hard, the sting of my tone running through him like an electric current, shocking him into replying with more desire. "i want to suck tiger's dick, Goddess, as i know it will please You."

"That's better. you're such a good boi, very good. Now, get on your knees and suck him, Damian."

Damian did as commanded, crawling over to where tiger was sitting, immediately kissing him as he fondled his dick, engaging deeper into the kiss as he relaxed and began stroking him in rhythm.

He moved to all fours, exposing his ass as he took tiger into his mouth.

tiger closed his eyes tightly, enjoying Damian's tongue, gripping the back of his head, encouraging him to continue.

I got so wet I took my fingers and rubbed them against my clit, feeling it swelling and getting harder by the second. Watching Damian's head moving with fervor as he completely immersed himself in his task, and the pure erotic look on tiger's face was enough to send me over the edge.

But I wanted something else first.

I moved behind Damian as he continued his pace, lubricant in hand, and began to coat his asshole with the cool liquid. I felt him clench for a few seconds, then relax as I massaged the hole and started to push my finger inside. I kept moving the lube inside of him, listening to him moan through the blow job he was performing. Before he could move to adjust, I slipped two more fingers inside of him.

He stopped for a few more seconds, moving his hips to grind against my fingers. My pulse quickened as I saw his body take my fingers and take them as deeply as he could.

Oh my God, this boy was getting me off and he didn't even know it!

I slid my fingers out of his ass, already in position to slide my strap-on inside of him, feeling my aggression becoming more intense. I pressed in slightly, teasing him, making him aware that something bigger was about to penetrate. I stopped every few seconds, to tease him a little more, but I wanted to see if he wanted it as badly as his body was telling me he did.

My answer came in Damian pushing back against me, gasping as my length slipped farther and deeper inside of him.

I could have come instantly, just from the sight of it. *Come on, pet, you can take it all. I can feel it, baby, you want to*, I silently cheered him on, wanting him to feel the change in me.

"Mmmm, good boi," I moaned while rubbing his cheeks. Before long, I had him filled completely, feeling his thighs resting against mine, his ass against my pelvis.

Damian shifted his hips, enjoying the fullness inside of him. He eventually began to rock his hips, rotating them slightly while slowly moving back and forth against me. I smacked his ass hard, reminding him of what he was supposed to be focusing on first, holding his hips in place to give him the clue I was still the one in control.

"Make tiger come, Damian," I commanded while rubbing and raking my nails down his back.

He moved with a speed that damn near made me jealous. tiger couldn't hold back much longer, holding the back of Damian's head as he desperately tried to wait to beg for release.

*"Ma'am, may i come, please? It feels so good, please?!?!?!"* tiger locked eyes with me, pleading with me that Damian was doing too good a job of getting him to climax.

"Come for him, tiger. Let him know how good he's been sucking you," I told tiger, barely resisting the urge to fuck him until after he was done with tiger.

Hearing tiger's familiar growl escape his lips was the sign I needed to let loose and violate Damian like tomorrow was not promised. I gripped his hips tightly, finding the groove I wanted to take my prey, plunging in and out, deeper and harder, giving no room for mercy or screaming from him.

Damian was caught in a complete typhoon, sweat pouring down

his body as his excitement found a fevered pitch he couldn't deny. I lost myself inside of the energy created between us, feeling him shake uncontrollably whenever I stopped to watch his body react to my assault.

"you want to come, don't you, slut?" I growled loudly.

"*Yes, Goddess, please, i want to come hard for You!*" Damian yelled, looking back at me.

I slapped his face immediately.

"*I didn't tell you to look at Me!*" I scolded, never letting up on the pace as I drilled deeper. "*Come on, baby, give Me that ass! Take My dick!*"

tiger moved to My shoulder, whispering in my ear, "May I suck him off while You fuck him, Goddess? i've been wanting to taste him for weeks, Ma'am, please?"

I nodded my approval as tiger moved under Damian, taking his hard shaft as deep as he could, wanting to feel him spurt all over his chest.

Damian clenched, trying hard to resist before his body gave in to what it wanted. "*Goddess, please let me come, please?!?!?!?!*"

His body shook against me, begging me for release.

"*Come, baby, come all over him!*" I commanded, feeling my own orgasm threatening to engulf me.

I heard the pitch from him that let me know the climax gripped him and refused to let him go. Damian gasped and moaned, almost willing himself not to scream.

"*Let it go, baby, you belong to Me now! Let it go!!!*" I yelled at him, determined to make him surrender.

"*Goddess, i'm coming!!!*" he finally yelled out, his eyes full of tears as the wave came crashing unmercifully over him. "i'm coming… i'm coming…oh, Goddess, it's so deep!"

I heard tiger under me, coaxing him on. "Give me your come, Damian! Mmmmm, damn, it's all over my chest!"

I felt dizzy from my climax consuming me, sliding out of Damian as tiger continued to milk him dry. I was on my back, trying hard to catch my breath, when I felt a tongue sliding furiously over my clit, driving me to the edge before I could protest.

"That's right; lick Her dry, bitch. Never let your Goddess go without coming!" I heard tiger yelling at Damian as he continued to lap fervently at my pussy. "That's it, keep going; make sure She knows you're thanking Her for letting you come!"

I let out a scream I was sure could have awakened the occult. I closed my eyes, unable to fight the intensity of the orgasms keeping their hold on me.

"*Stop!!!!*" I finally yelled out, unable to take any more.

I could barely open my eyes. I glimpsed tiger grab Damian by the neck and whisper something in his ear before pushing him back between my legs.

tiger moved to my ear, softly thanking me for the wonderful time before recovering to kneel beside me. "May i be released from Your service, Ma'am? i can send one of the service slaves in to help clean up, if it is Your command?"

I lifted Damian's head, staring at him deeply. I was so enthralled in the afterglow of being with him that I forgot tiger was still in the room with us. I placed Damian's head in my lap, turning my attention to tiger, who remained in his kneeling position until I spoke. "you are released from My service, tiger. It is My command for you to bring jezzabelle to Me, tiger. This bitch has earned a good fuck tonight, and she is exactly the slut to take care of him."

# THIRTY-TWO ⊗ SAJIRA

My body was on fire.

That wasn't exactly a bad thing.

I opened my eyes after feeling the effects of the chloroform wear off again, trying hard to get my bearings to figure out what time it was. I looked over at the clock, my eyes blurry, reading the time as well after one in the morning.

Over an hour had passed since this whole thing had happened.

The panic caused my heart to race as I tried to get my clothes together, wanting to get back to Daddy and Goddess ASAP because I knew they would be very upset we were gone for so long.

In my haste to find my clothes, I finally remembered shamise was with me during the whole scene.

I scanned the bedroom quickly, relieved my eyesight was clearing up, and found shamise on the other bed, still unconscious.

"shamise, baby, wake up." I nudged her. I worried she was too far gone and I feared I would have to get help if she didn't come to. After a few more moments, her body shifted and jerked, and she startled awake, trying to get her bearings quickly.

"sajira? Oh my God, what happened?" she asked me, her eyes locking with mine, trying to make some sense of where we were and what actually had happened.

It wasn't hard to figure that out.

The rape scene we secretly had begged for actually came to fruition. What's worse, it had happened without either Ramesses' or Neferterri's permission.

The punishment would be swift and severe once we had to explain where we were for the past ninety minutes.

"IT happened, sis," I explained to her, and her eyes widened as big as mine had when the fog finally had cleared. "Daddy and Goddess are gonna kill us over this."

shamise shook her head, then sighed as she nodded. "Yes, they probably will, but this is our fault, sis. we should have come clean to them in the first place about the fantasy, then we wouldn't have been caught in this mess."

I'd never been really punished before, at least not harshly, for something that had happened against my will. But I had to be honest with myself because I'd kept this from them, and they constantly told us that transparency was non-negotiable.

Tears immediately welled up in my eyes. "What are they going to do to us?"

"It doesn't matter, sis; the important thing is that we accept it with humility and grace, as they have taught us to do when that time would come," shamise told me. "It wasn't going to be all peaches and cream, baby."

Then this wicked smile crossed her lips, and I understood why she smiled that way. That was some of the most intense and primal sex I'd ever had, including my husband. I couldn't stop tingling, and my pussy was still wet from the thoughts of what we'd done came rushing through my mind.

We'd better hold on to those feelings while we still could.

It was time to pay the pipers.

☥

The walk back to the main building felt longer than it really was.

Our clothes weren't tattered, but they definitely looked like we'd been up to some carnal activities. The smirks on everyone's faces gave us the clue they really wanted to know what had happened. Some of the slaves tried to sneak looks while their Masters weren't looking to convey they wanted the exact same treatment that we'd just gotten.

I felt guilty as sin and remorseful as hell, but I couldn't stop tingling.

Damn, it repulsed me to have Deion inside of me, and I didn't want to feel that way. But yet, I secretly wished it could have lasted a little while longer.

shamise could see the smirk on my face, and she tapped my arm, scolding, "i know it was hot, sis, but it would help if we didn't let on to Daddy and Goddess just yet, okay?"

She was right, and I knew it.

As we approached the main building finally, I began to feel the tears begin again as the guilt began to creep back in.

Disobedience was not tolerated by our Masters.

The punishment wouldn't be physical, because they knew it would not have the desired effect. The mental torture would be more effective, and we both were aware of it.

The scene played out in my head like a horror movie.

We would be forced to recount the whole ordeal, every detail.

Then we would be asked if we liked what had happened to us, then admit we wanted it.

Then we would accept the punishment for such blatant disobedience and failure to follow the House rules regarding transparency.

God, I wasn't prepared for this, not yet.

We walked downstairs into the dungeon area, scanning the area to find where Ramesses and Neferterri were seated.

I stood still, confused we were able to find them in the exact seats we'd left them nearly two hours ago.

Something wasn't adding up. They would have normally sent their equivalent of the National Guard on the search if we were gone longer than thirty minutes.

"They're still where we left them, sis," I remarked to shamise.

"Yeah, i see that, too, baby." I saw the worried look on her face as she immediately dropped to her knees to crawl to where they were.

I followed her lead, crawling over to their seats, listening to them as they continued to converse with the audience surrounding them. shamise and I recently had begun the practice of alternating which of our owners we would kneel with if we left them simultaneously. This had shamise kneeling with Ramesses as I took my place at Neferterri's feet.

"There they are, finally." Neferterri smiled as she stroked my hair, moving to my cheek. "We were wondering whether you two had been kidnapped or something."

While the remark drew laughter from the group, I felt uneasiness from shamise. Looking over in her direction, I noticed she had a nervous smile on her face. Now I was really nervous about what could be happening, and my mind kept moving faster by the second.

Could they be that upset with us that they would put on such a display for the public?

I calmed myself down for a moment to remember the rules of the House, and I remembered Daddy and Goddess did not believe in public humiliation tactics, regardless of the transgression.

That calmed me, yet it scared me even more.

We would have to confess sometime before the night was out, so I kept a smile on my face and tried to bear through the anticipation until we were all alone to get this over with.

"No, Goddess, we were assisting the other NEBU slaves in entertaining guests," shamise answered gracefully. I knew I had a lot to learn then. She was as off-balance as I was, but she'd been in service to them longer, knowing the right words to say and making it look like nothing was wrong.

"That's My good girls, you should always set the example when you can." Ramesses kissed her forehead, turning to the crowd that was gathered around us. "Now, folks, if you will excuse us, we will leave you for the evening. If you have any issues, any of the Council members will be able to resolve them in our absence."

I smiled brightly as we took our leave, my mind moving to prepare for the interrogation that would soon arrive.

# THIRTY-THREE ✿ NEFERTERRI

"I've missed you, shamise."

Feeling her skin against mine, I felt like I was intoxicated all over again. Felt like the first time we took her so many years ago.

Raking my nails across her skin as she positioned herself on all fours, shamise swayed her hips, anticipating each delicious sensation from having not been touched by either of her Masters in nearly a year.

"If i am allowed to say so, my Goddess, i have missed You and Daddy terribly," she cooed, moaning as I smacked her ass.

Across from us, Ramesses and sajira were already in the throes of a primal scene, their growls and hissing filling the room. He'd already had his hands around her throat, growling in her ear as she writhed against him, trying to suppress the grin that threatened to spread across her lips.

shamise stared into my eyes, which I didn't mind her doing because the reconnection between us was long overdue and needed on levels I couldn't quite explain. All I knew was I had every intention to make her mine again.

Having the knowledge of the real reason for their disappearing act intensified the desire to take her and make her understand whom she belonged to. I had conflicting emotions within me, trying to decide if I wanted to interrogate her first and then ravage her, or keep on the path we were on already. My body already had voted, regardless of what my mind wanted, pulling her in to me to kiss her deeply.

I looked over at Ramesses and sajira, realizing he'd decided to do the same thing. There weren't too many problems a good orgasm couldn't fix, but this breach of protocol was going to take more than a good orgasm. Maybe two or three might do the trick.

"It seems your sis and Daddy are already a little busy." I grinned, watching them as they were oblivious to anything else being in the room with them. "I'm going to wear you out, shamise. I've wanted to do this for the last few weeks."

"Yes, my Goddess, i'm Yours to violate; my body belongs to You." shamise's response sent the familiar shivers down my spine, reminding me of how much I enjoyed the way she willingly gave herself to me.

I moved shamise onto her back, keeping her legs spread wide as I moved on top of her.

As she rotated her hips under me; I playfully slapped her face, trying to bring out the lioness in her. Both of the girls have cat-like tendencies, biting, scratching, all of the things that cats like to do when they're playful and in heat.

Both of our bitches were definitely in heat.

shamise's eyes were closed, so she didn't see that I'd had a surprise for her that would take our play time to the next level. The unfamiliar humming startled her, but I'd had her pinned against the bed with one hand while I brought out the source of her bewilderment.

The Hitachi Magic Wand…

I teased her clit with the vibrations, smiling as she bit her lip to try and stifle the scream.

"I didn't tell you that you couldn't scream, baby," I scolded, popping her lips as I said it. "I want you to scream, so scream, bitch."

"Oh my Goddess, that feels soooo good!" shamise let loose the minute the reins were taken off. Her body became more animated, feeling the vibrations of the Wand relentlessly taking her pleasure hostage. "Oh, Goddess, it feels so intense. my pussy is throbbing for You now!"

I kept the light pressure against her clit and outer lips, taking the Wand off to watch her body beg for the stimulation again. I loved how her body moved when she wanted to be fucked, and she didn't disappoint.

I heard sajira's screams getting louder by the second, her hissing and growling and moaning contributing to the extra wetness forming between my legs. Ramesses had her clothing completely off now, raking his nails across her chest and stomach, taking a small flogger, big enough to use in tight places, and rapidly slapping it against her clit, making sajira scream louder.

"Oh, Daddy, it's Yours, harder, please, harder!" I heard her screaming. "i'll be a good girl from now on, i promise!"

Now, I was curious as to what spurred that statement from sajira?

I felt shamise jerk for a second before her body went back into its rhythm, which let me know that she'd heard it, too, and it affected her as if something had happened between the two of them.

I was too caught up in my own lustful thoughts and actions to worry about it at the moment, but deep down I already knew what had happened. I didn't want to deal with the pang in my heart, but I was fine with things resolving themselves it in the morning.

Her essence radiated, her scent consumed us as I kept the pressure on her clit, waiting for her to explode at any moment.

"Oh, Goddess, may i come, please?!?!?!" shamise yelled out, her eyes closed tightly as if she were bracing for the coming storm. "It's right there, please, may i?"

Instead of answering her, I pushed her over the edge myself, a sadistic grin spreading quickly as her body bucked and her legs threatened to close, her defense mechanism when she's no longer in control of her orgasm.

I kissed her deeply as she moaned through the kiss, her body trembling under me, her hips still begging for the force the Wand provided. I took the Wand off her pussy, slipping one end the FeelDoe inside of my pussy, burying the shaft deep inside her as her orgasm continued its siege of her body, continuing the wave by pumping hard and fast inside of her.

Her eyes got wide when she realized I was inside her, tears flowing freely, no longer able to form audible words, and continued to sing in pitches and octaves as I kept the rhythm steady and fast, feeling the pressure building from the FeelDoe inside of me, stroking my G-spot, realizing my imminent orgasm would take me at any moment also.

I'd completely forgotten about my husband and our other slave, as my tunnel vision only focused on finding the next level of pleasure.

All that mattered was bliss.

I felt shamise clawing at my back, and I roughly pinned her hands over her head, looking deep inside her eyes, finding the place within her being reserved just for me. Call me a little selfish, but there were some things I knew belonged to Ramesses alone, and tonight was about carving that place for me within our beautiful, wonderful slave.

"I'm going to come, baby!" I yelled into shamise's ear, going faster to hasten the climax. "Oh fuck, you feel so good!"

I grabbed her so tightly when the wave began, I could have suffocated her. She instinctively wrapped her legs around my back, closing the connection between us more. I still had her hands pinned, feeling the energy flow between us, the passion that finally unlocked after so long apart.

"i'm Yours, Goddess…always Yours! Don't let me go, please!"

The climax subsided mercifully, and I lifted my head to lock eyes with shamise again. Her face glowed, and the smile on her face spoke more than any words we could say.

I had my shamise back, completely.

My senses began to flood back from the isolation I'd purposely shut out, hearing Ramesses and sajira reaching the crescendo of their own symphony.

I had no intentions of interrupting them, as I shifted my body to the side of shamise's, spooning her softly as we wrapped the covers over us, allowing the sensual sighs and moans escaping from sajira's mouth to serenade us as we entered the depths of the dream world.

Soon, morning would arrive, and the answers to the questions in my mind would come to fruition.

# THIRTY-FOUR ⊗ RAMESSES

The next morning was glorious.

Waking up in the master bedroom with all of my girls was indescribable. Yes, I'm a little spoiled when it came to this, especially when eventually we would have to send all the guests home and become parents, business owners, and vanilla again soon. I was missing Damian from the equation, but he was still with Jezzabelle, according to my Beloved, and as a man, I wasn't about to deprive another man of the pleasure she provided.

It still felt good, even if one was missing from the family.

But now there was business to attend to.

There were two hours the girls were unaccounted for that needed to be figured out, and only they would be able to recount. Last night would have been a good time to have that conversation, but I didn't want to ruin a perfectly decadent night to interrogate and punish the girls. Call me selfish, but I wanted what I wanted when I wanted it.

Being a Master could wait until morning; that was our collective conclusion.

Waking up to seeing three other female bodies intertwined with mine was something I hoped I would never get used to. It's rare we got to indulge like this. For the sake of the kids, it's best to wait until they'd matured a little more before we got into that type of conversation.

I was able to slip away from the women so I could be at peace with my thoughts and figure out what to do about the absence of the girls.

I would admit, I didn't think it would take that long, but sometimes you can't plan things like that. They are better off unscripted, as they tend to be the best scenes to witness.

I figured they simply needed some time alone to be together or something like that, but to be honest, I really wasn't feeling that thought pattern, either.

Oh well, Neferterri and I would find out once the girls woke up so we could deal with it accordingly.

Who was I kidding? I knew *exactly* what had happened last night while the girls were gone. So did my Beloved, but we weren't about to alert them until the proper moment.

My immediate thoughts drifted to the ring that rested next to my wedding ring and the rest of my jewelry.

*Master…*

Damn, it was a weird feeling to attribute my persona to that moniker. But I wasn't about to say I didn't earn this title, either.

The past three days or so was an exercise in running a gauntlet. I felt like every encounter with the other Masters was a test in disguise, trying to figure out if I was worthy of the respect and the reputation I'd taken such care to build.

My mind was taxed, but the end result had been more than worth the effort. My legacy was being cemented with each passing day as the compounds moved closer to completion, and I had the distinction of mediating the closure of a rift strained for a decade, an accomplishment none of the other Masters within the Society could claim.

Yet, it felt like I still had so much more to accomplish.

Maybe it was the warrior in me, always looking for the next

mission, the next conquest. Sometimes being still doesn't cut it.

I heard my women starting to stir, and I moved from my chair in the sitting room to the side of the bed where sajira and I made up the family pretzel, and nudged them all awake.

"Good morning, ladies." I grinned as they stretched to try and awaken and get their bearings. "We have business to attend to before brunch."

We all took quick showers so we could get to the heart of the matter, and I'm sure Neferterri felt the same tension on the girls as I did last night.

Something had happened to them, and they were very hesitant to tell us.

Neferterri had been on edge ever since the girls had left our sight, especially when they never wandered on the grounds without eyes on them. I'd had complete trust in the staff we'd put together, as they were people Dominic and I trusted implicitly.

The other things would fall into place.

I trusted that it would, and thankfully my trust was not misplaced.

♀

"we were raped last night."

Tears were in both of their eyes as they began to fully disclose what had happened to them while they were away from us.

"Well, we weren't 'raped,' exactly, but...it's hard to explain, Daddy." shamise was conflicted as to how to choose her words, not sure if they would anger us or if she were being exposed. "When we went to get sajira's belongings from the limo, we were drugged. I think it was chloroform."

My heart rate quickened. I felt like I was being told about some movie they'd gone to see while they were away, but it wasn't the case.

sajira continued, "When we woke up, we realized that we were still on the grounds, but couldn't figure out which one of the buildings we were in. we were blindfolded, but once one of the guys spoke, we knew it was Deion and an accomplice who had kidnapped us."

Neferterri's hands shook as she held on to shamise. "Go on, girls, We need to know everything."

"we were bound and stripped, and they didn't take off our blindfolds, even when things got rough," shamise told us. "It was scary, my Goddess, but it was…"

"It was, what, shamise?" I asked her, feeling sajira trembling under me from her spot at my feet. "Were you two hurt?"

"No, Daddy, that's what i was trying to say." she looked up at Neferterri, looking like she wanted this to be over. "There's something sajira and i have wanted to tell You, but we were too afraid to explain."

I raised an eyebrow, and Neferterri stared down at shamise, and then at sajira.

"What do you have to tell us?" Neferterri's tone in her voice could have stopped traffic.

"my Goddess, shamise and i confessed to each other that we had rape fantasies," sajira finally confessed, her tears flowing more now. "The men who kidnapped and took us, one of the guys was the 'phone Dom' that i had been talking to the past few weeks."

"you mean you broke the rules of your slut training?" Neferterri finally exploded. "How could you, both of you?"

"i'm sorry, Goddess, please forgive me." shamise sobbed through her words. "we were scared of what You would have thought of us if we told You."

Neferterri calmed down a little, trying to find a tone that wouldn't scare them any more than they already were. "you both know we are very disappointed in you. We have never given you a reason to suspect either your Daddy or I would shun you or make you feel less than what you are worth to us."

I just shook my head. "Had you come to us, at least one of us, we might have been able to find a way to make the scene happen for you, so you knew you would be safe as you indulged in your fantasy. Now, there's no possible way to duplicate that."

I looked at the girls, beside themselves with grief over having disappointed us, and what was worse, they did so while acting like they were amateurs who had never been trained before, treating us like they had no faith in us at all.

That hurt, and they needed to know that, period.

"We have drilled into you both a sense of transparency, that no matter what the disclosure, that we would deal with things together," I scolded them both. "The thing is Neferterri actually overheard the two of you confess to each other weeks ago while you were caring for our leathers. We usually review the House surveillance cameras during the week to make sure the kids haven't gotten into anything they shouldn't have. Imagine Her surprise in hearing you two conspiring to breach protocol?"

A look of embarrassment washed over their faces, perhaps forgetting the walls do indeed have ears at the House.

"your Goddess came to Me to let Me know of the information you'd confessed, and we waited until you made up your minds to let us know." I kept going, setting up for the surprise I had in store for them. "After a week, when neither of you came to us to say anything, we were forced to take other measures to get what we needed to know out of you."

"What do You, mean, my Master?" sajira queried, ready to panic.

"Hello, ladies," Deion's voice traveled from the sitting room. "Did you miss me?"

The screams from the girls were priceless, if not ear-splitting. Their eyes told us they didn't know what to make of the situation.

Dominic walked from around the doorway that separated the bedroom from the sitting room. In his hand was a voice synthesizer he'd been using to disguise his voice. He and I knew the girls would have recognized his real voice, so we created "Deion" to throw them off, while I fed him information and trained him how to act to break down sajira's defense mechanisms.

Until this very moment, neither of them had a clue it was him the whole time.

"Oh my God!" shamise screamed again. "But how did You...why?"

"Because we had to teach you a lesson for keeping something like this from us," Neferterri retorted. "We planted Dominic as your 'phone Dom' to keep control of the situation, to make sure you didn't get hurt. Do you realize how much harm would have really come to you if complete strangers had taken you?"

I walked Dominic to the door so he could check on the guests downstairs. Brunch was due to begin in about twenty minutes, and I didn't want us to be late.

sajira wanted to scream again, but the shock had finally worn off. I think she and shamise had finally figured out what Neferterri meant. Had this been an actual stranger, like the jackass that tried to prank-call me before the event, things could have gone a lot differently.

The look in their eyes was the confirmation we needed that the message had been driven home.

"Master, my Goddess, please accept our apologies for disobeying the rules of the House." shamise rocked back and forth in her kneeling position as she formally asked for forgiveness. "we should not have tried to do this on our own, and we both realize this now."

Neferterri's eyes softened; seeing the girls so earnestly remorseful was enough to grant the request. "you are both forgiven, shamise, sajira. Now, I want you both to take a look at something."

The further looks of confusion only inspired grins from Neferterri and me.

She reached over to the nightstand and turned on the television. She switched the output settings, which put a closed-circuit television on the screen.

"Do you recognize the room, girls?" Neferterri asked. Our slaves blushed profusely.

"Yes, Goddess, that was the room we were in," sajira affirmed.

Neferterri pressed the play button on the remote, and the whole scene began to unfold, live and in living color and with extremely clear sound.

I watched their faces move from horror to sheer pleasure as they saw themselves on video. sajira unconsciously licked her lips as she moved closer to my body to enjoy the show. I watched shamise move closer to Neferterri, burying her head in Neferterri's chest like she had let loose the teenager inside of her, trying to not believe it was really her on the screen.

After moving to the end of the scene, shamise was much more comfortable seeing the scene. She was still slightly trembling at her Goddess's feet, but she wasn't as innocent as she was ten minutes ago.

Neferterri clicked off the video after the image of shamise kicking the other guy's balls and the girls being drugged again ended the video replay. "So, what did we learn, girls?"

"we will never keep anything from You again, my Goddess," they replied in unison.

I checked the clock, realizing we had about five minutes to get down to the dining room to greet our guests and send them on their way home.

"Remember, we are always watching, girls," I explained to them. "If we have in within our power, you will always have eyes on you. We love you that much."

"Oh, but don't think for a moment that you won't be punished for breaking the rules, girls. Yes, you're forgiven, but that doesn't mean there aren't consequences for your behavior, either." Neferterri's expression was stone-cold serious. My eyes never left them as I noticed their heads bow, and they transitioned to their bowing positions, to show respect even when being chastised. "We have guests to see about, but make no mistake, we have a lot of talking and training to ensure this never happens again. Now, rise, My sexy girls, it's time to take care of business."

As the ladies left, Dominic and I had a quick moment to chat before following them into the dining hall. "Go ahead, say it, I'm waiting," Dom blurted. "You said it would go down like this, and I was wrong."

He noticed the smirk on my face before I crafted my reply. "I'm not about to say, 'I told You so,' Dom, but I will say this: I've been doing this a long time. You'll learn where I'm coming from in due time, but for now, let's finish things so we can take the rest of the week off, shall we?"

# THIRTY-FIVE ⊗ EPILOGUE

"Thank you all for coming."

We finally made it down to the dining room, greeting all who wanted our attention, watching in awe at the crowd that had taken advantage of the accommodations on the grounds and wanted to take part in the brunch festivities.

At His space, also waiting to greet us was Amenhotep, grinning at the familiarity of the ritual that I had taken great pains to duplicate as much as I could. paka was at His feet, suppressing a smile of her own, which warmed my heart, as they were the only two I truly cared if the festivities were to their liking.

Even though this was nearing the middle of the summer, I enjoyed the holiday feel of the morning. The mimosas were being brought out with fervor by the NEBU slaves, the main buffet table was stocked as heavily as in past occasions with pastries and fruits, and breakfast foods were also loaded, for those that might have worked up an appetite before attending.

"I'm not saying anything, except to say the Lady of NEBU will say a few words first." I looked at my Beloved, who blushed to some degree, even though I'd already told her beforehand she would lead the brunch for this special occasion.

She kissed me slightly, giving me a look that said, *I'm going to kill you later.*

"Ladies and gentlemen, Beloved and I would like to thank you all for coming down to help us with the grand reopening of NEBU," Neferterri began as sajira and shamise took their positions on either side of us, and Damian knelt beside her other hip. "I am pleased the evening turned out to be such a grand success. It is a sign of some good things to come, and we are proud to announce a few things this morning to be spread to your respective communities."

She looked in the direction of Master Seti first, raised her glass toward him, and stated, "Master Seti and the contingent up in the D.C./Maryland/Virginia area will be overseeing the compound in that area, *Thebes*. We want to thank Him for His assistance with that project."

After the applause died down, Neferterri turned to me to continue the announcements.

I was drinking my mimosa when she decided to turn things over to me, and I nearly choked on my drink, which inspired a chuckle out of Amenhotep first, and then spreading through the rest of the audience.

I looked toward Master Osiris and Lady Hatshepsut, raising my glass in their direction. "Master Osiris and Lady Hatshepsut are taking care of the project we are beginning out in the Las Vegas area, the *Temples of Deshret*. I am sure the Los Angeles and San Francisco areas will be very excited to have a private compound to call their own also."

More applause, like the news was something long overdue. Amenhotep was the loudest of the audience, enjoying the fruits of his plan coming together. I cracked my own smile, more from relief all of the buildup had finally been completed, and without too much drama, at least for now.

Finally, now that Damian was in his place, and after last night's performance Neferterri told me about while the girls were away, now was as good a time as any.

"Now that the formalities are out of the way, I have a personal announcement to make." I waited for the crowd to calm down. "Damian, as a few of you know, has been training within the House, earning his way into the mix. After receiving various kudos from several attendees last night on his performance, both professionally and intimately, it is our pleasure to announce Damian will be given his training collar, and his name will be recognized within the community as amani."

The look on his face was one for the books.

Neferterri bent down and kissed his forehead, and sajira and shamise hugged him tightly, happy over the surprising news.

"Okay, folks, I'm out of any more news at this time. I want you all to know we had a wonderful time with you, please enjoy the ride home, and our drivers will make sure you get to your destinations in one piece."

♀

"You did all right, youngster."

It's funny how hearing those words from someone you respect highly does certain things to you. Hearing those words from Amenhotep was like music to my ears, especially after four months of having to go back and forth with Him concerning the schematics and having him sign off on everything.

That was the detail I'd left out when it came to explaining everything to the other members when I pitched the other compounds. It had to look like the whole idea was mine to resurrect the compounds or else the plans would have hit a stalemate, especially with Seti.

Amenhotep figured that there might not have been as much resistance if I brought the idea up this time around. As I found out throughout the night, Osiris and Seti, despite their differences at the time, were absolutely against the idea of a compound at all, saying that it would bring too much attention to the Society, and they were comfortable with the anonymity of it all.

I will admit, operating under the radar does have its perks, but in the Information Age, there's simply no such thing as privacy anymore.

I guess, in the end, even dinosaurs had to adapt or they would find themselves extinct.

"Thank You, Sir, but I couldn't have pulled this project off without You." I shook His hand as we headed out to the gazebo by the pool to enjoy the unexpected coolness of an Atlanta summer afternoon. "Last night turned out very well on a lot of fronts."

"I've heard about the security firm You started with Dominic also, kid. I'm impressed, and I'm sure Your father is proud You've come full circle and put Your true skills to some good use."

I cracked up on the security reference, but he was right; some things do come naturally.

"That wasn't too hard to set up, Sir, and I have some good people working under Dom and Me," I bragged. "I think it will serve a good purpose, and it might fill a need that's been lacking in the community for a while now."

"Well, there's no need to rest on Your laurels just yet, Ramesses," Amenhotep pointed out, sitting down on the bench as we watched the male service slaves working on the pool and cleaning the water. "Are Your immunizations up to speed?"

"I hate it when You get all cryptic and cloak and dagger, Sir." I rolled my eyes and exhaled. I had just helped pull off the mother of all openings within the kink community, even set up another business, and He's already talking about the next big thing. "Just spit it out, already."

"I want You to take a trip with Me, youngster," Amenhotep directed. "I'll give You a few weeks to get everything in order, and then after that, I want You to block out about three weeks so we can take care of something overseas. Something I've been cooking up since I moved to the island."

"Can I at least know where You're talking about, since we're talking about going overseas?" I was ready to strangle Him, but the funniest thing was I did the same thing to my employees at the firm, including Dominic.

There's a method to His madness, and His track record let me know I could trust the direction He was trying to head in.

"Yeah, I guess I can let You know what's going on." Amenhotep stroked His beard as He sized me up for my reaction, then answered my question with a question of His own. "How would You like to create our own version of Hedonism?"

# ABOUT THE AUTHOR

Shakir Rashaan currently lives in suburban Atlanta with his wife and two children. Rashaan's catalog includes the *Chronicles of the Nubian Underworld (The Awakening: Book One, Legacy: Book Two, and Tempest: Book Three), Deviant Intent (OBSESSION, DECEPTION, and RECKONING)*, and a collaborative novel series with Anna J, *Motives*. Other credits include several anthologies, including *Erotic Snapshots Vols. 5 & 6, Lies Told in the Bedroom, and Zane Presents Z-Rated: Chocolate Flava 3*. You can see more of Rashaan at http://www.shakirrashaan.com.